Praise for Stig Saeterbakken

"*Siamese* is a difficult and brilliant book, like one of those skulls inscribed "As I am now, so shall you be" that a death-besotted Romantic might have kept by his bedside."

—Jim Krusoe, *The New York Times*

"Saeterbakken skillfully creates a delightful, solipsistic tension between the querulous old couple. Their kinship is a lovely, bitter riot."

—*Publisher's Weekly*

T0244678

Other Books by Stig Saeterbakken in English Translation

Novels

Self-Control
Through the Night

SIAMESE

BY
STIG SAETERBAKKEN

TRANSLATED BY
STOKES SCHWARTZ

DALKEY ARCHIVE PRESS
Dallas, TX / Rochester, NY

Deep Vellum | Dalkey Archive Press
3000 Commerce Street
Dallas, Texas 75226
www.dalkeyarchive.com

Copyright © 1997 by J.W. Cappelens Forlag AS
Originally published in Norwegian as *Siamesisk* by J.W. Cappelens Forlag AS, 1997
Translation copyright © 2010 by Stokes Schwartz

Second Dalkey Archive Press Edition, 2024
All rights reserved.

Support for this publication has been provided in part by grants from the National Endowment for the Arts, the Texas Commission on the Arts, the City of Dallas Office of Arts and Culture, the Communities Foundation of Texas, and the Addy Foundation.

 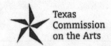

Paperback ISBN: 9781628976021
Ebook ISBN: 9781628975994

Library of Congress Cataloging-in-Publication Data
Saeterbakken, Stig, 1966- [Siamesisk. English]
Siamese / Stig Saeterbakken ; translated by Stokes Schwartz, p. cm.
ISBN 978-1-56478-325-7 (pbk .: alk. paper)
I. Schwartz, Stokes. II. Title.
PT8951.29.A39S5313 2010
839.82'374—dc22
2009028130
Cover design by Daniel Benneworth-Gray
Interior design by Douglas Suttle

Printed in Canada

SIAMESE

THE FLUORESCENT TUBE in the bathroom light was burned out when I went in to see him that morning. Naturally, he hadn't noticed anything. When I opened the door, he was sitting in the pitch-dark and chewing gum as usual. The light from the hallway fell diagonally into the room, cutting him in two—I could see the back of his chair and the back of his head, nothing else. The heap of foil gum wrappers on the floor glittered and looked as though it was swirling, a lethargic whirlpool.

"You again?" he asked. I thought at first that I should mention the light, but let it go. It would just be bothering him unnecessarily.

"Do you realize what you've done?" he roared. "What you've ruined?" Then I heard him shout something about his concentration, but by then I was on my way out of the bathroom to call the super. I left the door open, I don't know why—or maybe I do. It's because I can't get used to acting as though he isn't there. I tell myself that it doesn't make any difference, but this never helps. I always feel like it would be worse than burying him alive if I switched off the light whenever I left the bathroom. I don't know. Maybe I'm just superstitious, but I worry he would probably drop dead if I left him sitting in the dark for too long.

I dialed the number that Edwin had once written on a slip of paper and pinned to the wall above the telephone. We have a new building superintendent, but the number's still the same. He answered after a single ring, and I was glad to hear that his voice was clear and distinct. I didn't need to ask him to repeat anything he said. At first, I wasn't sure what I should tell him. I'd called without thinking of anything beforehand, but I finally managed to spit it out, what the problem was. He said that he would come up right away, and I said back that it would be terrific if he could. But I regretted this as soon as I hung up. It occurred to me that I'd absolutely never expected him to come so quickly. I'd actually hoped for a little time to straighten up the apartment and take care of a few things before he arrived. But it was too late to think about that now. It didn't really matter. Surely he wouldn't care what the apartment looked like. For him this would be just another little job to take care of. Surely changing a bulb in a bathroom only takes a couple of seconds. Hopefully. For Edwin's sake. I can never decide what the best course of action is—whether I should ignore him, act like he isn't even there, or try to include him in what's going on. And then I always end up feeling ridiculous for having worried about the question in the first place. That it was ever a problem for me.

Is it too cold in there for Edwin, still just wearing his jogging suit?

The super was younger than I expected. Much younger. I was a little confused when I opened the door. I hesitated a bit before I let him in. It was the first time I'd seen him up close. He had on a blue windbreaker and glasses. A couple of white paint flecks on his eyeglass frames gave him a slightly disheveled look—that was my first impression of him—though his glasses were otherwise well maintained and, for all I knew, even rather expensive. He didn't say anything, and he didn't introduce himself, which disappointed me. I'd been looking forward to hearing his high, clear voice again.

"It's in here," I said and showed him the way. I could tell that he wanted to get right to work without any small talk. A faint smell hung in the air behind him, aftershave or deodorant. A clean smell. I pushed open the bathroom door for him, and he opened a yellow banana-shaped bag and pulled out a flashlight. He turned it on and shined it into the room without going in. Like he thought he was standing on the edge of a cliff. The light fell on Edwin, who had turned himself away from the door—he hadn't known anyone was coming—and his neck looked like a dried root. The super looked at me, and I didn't know what I should say. So I went into the bathroom with him. He pointed his light up toward the fixture in the ceiling, which was full of tiny, black shadows on the inside. Edwin belched then, and this startled the custodian, who dropped his flashlight. It fell to the floor with a bang and the darkness came back, covering us like a heavy curtain—I'd closed the door behind us without thinking. Edwin belched again—I was a little startled myself—and started to give out a stink. Then the flashlight came on again, right in Edwin's face, but he didn't even blink. His eyes looked like they were made of plastic. The super found a place to set down his flashlight, angling it in such a way that he was able to direct as much light as possible up toward the ceiling. I said that I would leave the rest to him, knowing that I would only be in the way if I stayed in the bathroom. I mentioned that there was a step stool in the hall if he needed something to stand on. I left the door open on my way out, thinking that maybe this would be best for the young man, since it was his first time in our bathroom. I could only imagine what he was thinking.

I hurried to the kitchen and put on a pot of coffee, extra strong, like I thought he would prefer it, found some Christmas cake in the bread box, cut several pieces, and put them on the dish with the little blue stem. I took the dish into the living room and set out cups on the coffee table that had been left to us by

Edwin's mother. I had to dust the cups a bit with a dish towel first. I smoothed out the tablecloth and lit some candles. The wax was thick around the wicks, so I had to be careful lighting them without burning my fingers. I peeked into the bathroom. The super had taken the step stool from the hall and he was standing on it with his arms outstretched, either screwing the old bulb out or the new bulb in. The shadows on the bathroom walls stretched up, coming to a point, looking ominous. I thought I heard voices. Were the super and Edwin talking? Edwin had been quiet while I was in the bathroom, which was what I expected. I had difficulty believing that he would have struck up a conversation with this young man. Most likely, Edwin just wanted to be left alone again as soon as possible. I went back out to the kitchen and got the coffee—I listened but didn't hear anything—put the coffeepot on a tray, took it to the table, and then went back to the bathroom. The super was just climbing down from the step stool and moving to the light switch by the door. A couple of seconds later, everything was in order again. I clapped my hands several times to let him know that I thought he had done a wonderful job. I went over to Edwin, who was sitting exactly as before, face turned away, neck bent, and touched him on the shoulder. The slick material of his jogging suit felt like silk.

"So, my dear," I said, "now you've got light in your room again." The super had gathered up his things and was standing there with his bag in his hand, looking a bit lost. "Good work," I said to him, "really good work." And it really was—it made everything brighter in there. The faucets shined like candelabras. "Imagine having such talent at such a young age," I said, partly to myself, but mostly for his benefit. I shook my head to show how impressed I was.

He indicated that he had to leave. "Hey," I said to him, "there's something else I'd like to ask you to have a look at . . . while you're here." I wanted to make it seem as though this really was the most convenient time for it. I walked ahead, out to the kitchen, so he would follow me. He seemed like a considerate man. I asked him to open the refrigerator door, which he did. It was completely dark inside. He understood at once what the problem was—I didn't need to explain anything. He opened his bag again—clearly it held everything a man could possibly need—and mumbled something that I couldn't quite understand. Did he only speak clearly on the telephone? And while I stood and waited, he changed the little bulb. He pressed the little button next to it several times to demonstrate that everything was working now, exactly as it should. Before he shut the door, he stuck his hand into the freezer. Was that to check the temperature? I don't know, but it was a good thing he did, because then he took the time to adjust the thermostat.

"My goodness!" I said. I like it when people do a little bit more than they've been asked to. He smiled . . . broadly? "Do you have a little time for a cup of coffee before you go?" I asked, and it seemed to me—though I can't be sure—that the question came as a complete surprise to him. Surely he'd noticed the set table on our way to the kitchen?

I poured some coffee into a cup and offered him some Christmas cake. The super ate like he'd been starving—and then it occurred to me that the slices I'd cut were perhaps unnecessarily thin: a good slice of cake can be a good meal—and he emptied his coffee cup in two gulps, though that's really nothing to complain about, since our white cups don't hold very much. He didn't say a thing. He hadn't said anything, in fact, since we'd sat down at the table, only eaten and drank. But now he was refusing more cake and just sitting there. This puzzled me. If I hadn't known any better, I would have thought that he was waiting to be paid. But maybe this behavior was typical of supers? I wanted to think of something to ask him that would keep him here for a bit longer. I knew that he painted a bit in addition to his professional duties. He had a room in the basement that he had converted into a studio. According to Finborud, who lives right over the basement, the whole place smells like turpentine whenever the super is down there painting. In addition, there had been complaints from the other tenants to the effect that our super seemed to be taking too much advantage of his position. They felt that being able to live here rent-free and not have to pay a telephone bill ought to be enough to satisfy anyone. But he was a nice guy, and it seemed the tenants were more or less pleased with him. Although he'd only been here a short time, the super was always eager to help, and almost always home when you called. But he also seemed—I don't know why—like a rather lonely person. Last summer he wore a multicolored sun hat and mowed the lawn with a gasoline-powered riding mower, which you drive like a car. It was obvious that he thought it was fun. He seemed extremely content. He took his time doing it.

"So, you're also a painter," I said. He nodded, a bit sadly—perhaps because he didn't have enough time for painting, thanks to his responsibilities; or maybe it was because he wasn't happy with what he'd achieved up to this point? Who knows. I'd had to say something. Maybe I should have said something else. "Well, is painting pictures any harder than painting staircases?" I tried to make this sound like an invitation, so that he would feel like talking a bit about his work. It's hard to show interest in a subject you know next to nothing about. But he just smiled. Was there also a hint of disdain? I wasn't sure. I sat and waited for him to say something. I couldn't look away. But now it didn't seem like he'd meant to be unkind. I wondered how old he was. There was something simultaneously adult and quite childish about him, as if he knew exactly what he needed to know, but not any more than that.

"Of course it takes time," I said. I couldn't come up with anything better. Then he looked up at me, as if asking a question, but I didn't hear what he said—if he said anything. I wasn't entirely sure. Was he mumbling on purpose? "What?" I asked, in a deliberate ambiguous tone. "With your job I mean," I added. Perhaps that's what he needed. A clarification. I thought later that what had seemed so youthful about him was the fact that he sat there kind of defiantly, even though we didn't know each other, waiting until something got said that actually interested him before bothering to answer. He set down his cup, took out a pack of cigarettes, helped himself to one, and lit it without asking permission. This was fine. The unfamiliar scent of tobacco that filled the room was refreshing. He watched the orange glow that followed every drag. It seemed he would be content to do this for hours. He went on sitting silently, a bit hunched in his jacket, which was a little too big for him, and which had dark brown buttons that looked like snail shells—small, silent conquerors of the shiny surrounding material.

Then he spoke, and his voice was just as clear and distinct as it had been on the telephone: "I'm going to paint a picture of a dog for Mrs. Gustafsen."

"Really?" I said, and for one reason or another, I could immediately see the picture he would paint in my mind.

"Yes, she's given me a photo, so I have something to base it off of." I wondered whether I should ask him if it was difficult to paint pictures that really looked like their subjects, but I wasn't sure if this was the right thing to say. I felt like anything I could say might somehow offend him.

"She said that she'd pay me well," he added and shrugged his shoulders like it didn't really mean very much to him—the money, not the picture. It was possible that he saw the assignment as something that was beneath him, but at the same time it was clear that he was pleased someone had asked him for a painting. I could imagine, since he had mentioned it, that he didn't get requests like this very often, although he tried to pretend that it was something he was used to. He put out his cigarette in his coffee cup, but that was my fault. I hadn't thought to put out an ashtray. We stayed seated for a moment, neither of us saying anything. Then a scream, like a scream of fear, came from the bathroom. The young man jumped a little but tried to act nonchalant. It was quiet for a moment, but then another scream followed. It sounded like someone was trying to pull Edwin's tongue out. The super looked up at me, our eyes met—equally wide—and what I saw in them was despair, a deep despair. I was sure of it. So much despair it made him feel helpless. So helpless he couldn't hide his despair.

What was it about his misery that made me feel so cheerful? Because that's what I was, all of a sudden—cheerful—I can't find any other word for it; a happiness, a sudden trembling happiness flowed through me, even bringing tears to my eyes. I looked at the young man with gratitude—I didn't know what to say. Surely he would have liked to stand up and leave, but it seemed like he couldn't. There was something preventing him.

Finally he asked, "How can he just sit in there all the time?" He looked away as he said this, but it was clear his question had been meant for me. I smiled. Of course, I had expected that he would ask something like that—my voice quavered as I replied that Edwin was an old man, and that it's different for an old man, as opposed to someone as young as himself. The super nodded, a wrinkle forming between his eyebrows. I noticed that he had scars from chicken pox—surely not a recent outbreak?—but it seemed like the young man was, if not especially interested, then curious at least, in a strange and somewhat reluctant way.

"It's not easy taking care of my husband all the time," I volunteered, a bit unsure about how much I should say. The super didn't answer—but I hadn't thought he would: it wasn't so important what he said, or if he didn't say anything at all, just so long as he didn't see things in a negative light, in case I did decide to confide in him.

"No," I said, "it's not very easy." But I didn't say anything else. I worried that if I started telling him about how it is, I wouldn't be able to stop, and what might come out wouldn't necessarily be good. I also knew that I'd regret most of what I said, so it was probably best not to say anything . . . I don't know . . .

Edwin's voice came from the bathroom.

"Erna? *Eeeeeernaaaaaah?*"

It sounded mournful, wasn't the screech that he'd let out earlier, wasn't even loud enough that I couldn't have avoided hearing it entirely if I'd been in the kitchen busy with something else. So I chose not to hear him. But it puzzled me that he'd called. Did he think the young man had left?

The super—I'd forgotten all about him for a second—sat and nodded his head. I couldn't help but feel he wasn't actually listening to anything I said. Was his friendly attention nothing more than common courtesy? I asked if he wanted a little more coffee, but maybe I shouldn't have done that, because he said no thank you and that he had to go. There were other things waiting for him, as he put it. He stood up.

"Well, thank you again," I said. "I know how it goes—there's always something that needs taking care of," I added, to show him that I didn't think his "other things" were only some kind of excuse. I followed him out. He hesitated a bit when we went past the bathroom door—it was like he couldn't bring himself to leave without saying something else about my situation. Maybe he was looking for something to say that wouldn't seem forced? Or maybe he was wondering whether or not he ought to duck into the bathroom and say his goodbyes? But the door was locked. He went on, quietly, uncertainly.

"Hey," I said, and then found myself unsure of what I'd wanted to say. He stopped.

"Did you speak to him?" I asked. "While you were in there?"

I knew I had to choose my words carefully now. "I mean, did he say anything to you?" The super stood there with a slightly blank look on his face.

"With me and him, it's always the same old stuff," I added, "so I was just curious whether or not he said anything to you." It was a while before the super answered—so long that when he finally responded with a no, saying that Edwin hadn't said anything to him, there was no mistaking his internal conflict, and likewise that it was important for him not to give this away. In a sense, I was glad. There was something refreshing about his loyalty to Edwin. At the same time, I saw how silly it had been of me to ask in the first place. It must have made me seem like a nosy, awful person. The super opened the front door. I wanted to say something before he left that would leave a better impression on him. He started down the staircase like someone with all the time in the world. The exaggerated letters printed on his tool bag, slanted to convey rapid motion, didn't quite match his casual pace. It occurred to me that if he disappeared now, I would never be sure—once I shut the door—if he'd ever really been here.

"I hope Mrs. Gustafsen likes the dog you're going to paint for her!" I shouted down the stairs. It echoed a bit strangely out there in the hallway, I have to admit.

THE MIND IS a place for reflection, but also a place for suffering. It's a dark hole full of words. A pure hell. But the rest of me isn't really worth discussing. I'm like Diogenes, who lived in a barrel. This body is my barrel. It's about as long and about as roomy. It's found a comfortable position for itself. There's still some life in it. No more than what I need to get through the day. A few heartbeats, a few breaths, you really can't ask for more . . . I don't have emotions when I think, which is an improvement.

I don't become sad, and I don't laugh either, even if I happen to remember something I used to think was funny. I prefer to avoid laughing whenever possible. I don't recognize my own laughter. It gives me the chills whenever I hear it. Of course, I belch from time to time, but there's nothing I can do about that. The burps just bubble up my throat, like rabbits out of a hat . . .

I also don't have sensations when I think. The pain is gone. It's like I'm sitting here with a block of ice between my legs. I'm so numb down there, that part of me might as well be declared dead, though it would be an exaggeration to say that the rest of me is alive and in good health. I have at least finished with something, finished ahead of time, before the great labor begins, when everything will vanish . . .

What will it be like, that day when the plug is pulled, when life slurps down the drain like some stinking, leftover soup? I think about it once in a while. I hope that my head is clear enough that day for me to recognize what's happening. It's not every day that you get to see something like that . . .

Will I catch myself crossing over to the other side when this life ends and another begins? Will I hear any special sounds? A tiny creak, maybe, or a violent crash? It would be best if things just ended with an inconsequential little click. But in any case, there's certainly not going to be anyone waiting for me on the other side, standing there to take my hand and welcome me in. No, there won't be anyone there to orient me, run through the local regulations with me, no, that much I'm sure of . . .

When it comes to death, you should be prepared for anything. I won't have any grand illusions about it, myself, or the life I've lived, on the day I lose it. Yes, a man ought to die the same way that he's lived. Something I've always believed. And still do. It's important to be consistent . . .

I don't want to leave anything behind, aside of course from my own remains. An ice-cold little body, dried up and sunken in like some hideous troll, an empty bag, and they can do what they want with it, the ones who come to clean up after me, burn it, or bury it in the earth, or chop it up into tiny pieces and feed it to the pigs. I'm not against being used for something useful . . .

I mentioned it to De-Sarg once. He said that it sounded like I'd become stuck on a very philosophical attitude toward death. I replied that I didn't know a thing about that stuff . . .

Most of the people at Kronsæther died believing an elegant lie. They were stuffed full of all the usual nonsense when the end was near. It was, of course, intended as a kind gesture on the parts of the soon-to-be bereaved, always keeping an eye on the inheritances waiting for them under their loved ones' clammy sheets. Yes, once in a while there would be someone in the family, usually someone a bit younger than the rest, who would insist on being absolutely frank with their dying relative right until the end. But, as a rule, the truth was usually set to one side, since time was so short. The dying were allowed, as a last privilege, to fool themselves in whatever ways pleased them the most. So, they were allowed to dwell on memories of rich and exciting lives. These final hours of comfort naturally meant more to them than any consideration of what was right or wrong . . .

The border between right and wrong is fluid, like that between life and death. Oh yes, I know what to expect. Ten doctors will stand around my deathbed just to say, "Aha, now he's really done for, the old bastard!" at completely different times, depending on which body part they've put their money on breaking down first. But it doesn't do any good to remind myself. Now of all times. For all I know, my intestinal worm is running rampant. I lost all feeling in my feet ages ago. I only get up and move around on them now and then for a change of pace. Beyond that, I don't know a thing about them anymore. Just that they're down there, someplace, at the end of my body. Maybe half eaten up, for all I know, white and sweaty, with gaping holes where my wandering worm slithers in and out, perhaps gnawing in toward the bone at this very moment, gorging itself on my carcass under the happy misconception that I've already died, since why else would I be sitting so still . . .

Oh no, I have my bedroom slippers on. That's what that is. A little thing, but still, she knows I hate bedroom slippers. The bitch knows. I remember the day she bought them for me. She unwrapped them in here. They crinkled in pretty tissue paper, and she couldn't contain her excitement. She was almost hysterical when she told me about them. She described the slippers for me at great length, large and gray or something, felt or something, the kind of thing your feet can't breathe in, with embroidered edgework all the way around the sole. I remember her whole description. She might just as well have stuffed them down my throat . . .

I had a pair of shoes once. Where are they now? I don't know. They were leather, black, with rubber soles, so I was also able to wear them in the winter. They were good shoes, and I walked to work in them. I walked home in them. I hardly ever took them off. All the other shoes I tried felt like they had screws in them, boring up into my feet. These I used year round. Tiny rocks rattled around in the soles, souvenirs from the landscape I tramped through when I went out in the spring. These shoes felt solid, secure in a way. When I had them on, I inevitably glanced at the footwear of any people I met, judging them according to the kind of shoes they wore . . .

The worst was the head nurse, that old bat. She had these awful contraptions, some kind of flip-flops, like shower clogs, full of little nubs, supposedly massaging her feet as she walked. When we had meetings, she would sit there rubbing her feet back and forth over the floor in them. She couldn't get enough. The one advantage of those shoes was that they always let people know when she was nearby. They made a kind of snapping noise against the floor when she walked, almost like the crack of a whip . . .

She didn't give me any kind of warning ahead of time. One day she just showed up and told me that she'd bought them. I didn't feel a thing when she put those slippers on me. It was like my legs had been dunked in ice water. I can't remember if she's come by since and taken them off again. They're probably still there . . .

I smell like a corpse. Who knows how long I've been decomposing. I think there's more ammonium chloride than flesh down there now. I don't know whether I'd be able to find my cock even if I tried. My fingers are swollen and numb. They have no feeling in them for days at a time. Once, a tiny flame burned. I don't remember when it was put out, and I don't remember how it felt when it burned. Now, the thing just hangs there like a trophy.

It has a plastic hose threaded through the opening. I'm sitting here with my cock in an endlessly long condom, my last defense against something that, otherwise, would certainly have devoured me. It's like an umbilical cord connected to a stillborn child . . . It's good that it never let out any offspring. Children shouldn't have to see their parents like this. My father was clever. He left everything behind at the age of fifty-five, when he escaped by losing his mind. He escaped having to lose his teeth. He escaped the smell of his own gums as they rotted. He escaped being reduced to a filthy little pig, which was how everyone ended their days at Kronsæther, everyone together, equal, whether they had been a priest or a cabin boy in life . . . They had no interest in hygiene. They all sat around scratching their crotches while they ate. It seemed like they began to shrink almost as soon as they arrived up there. They became smaller and smaller, more and more like themselves as they'd been as children. The very oldest residents looked like fetuses. One of the girls came by once and showed me how big Pedersen in room fourteen was, and she used exactly the same gestures as someone indicting the size of a fish they caught recently . . .

There's always some filth. Regardless of one's circumstances. But I was determined that it would never get that bad with me. This was my goal. I decided on it when I began to lose my eyesight quite young. It started with some tiny spots on my retinas: first a couple, then several. They resembled small grains of oats. They began to mat themselves together into larger clumps after a few years, mostly in the right eye. At first, it wasn't so bad. In normal daylight, everything just seemed a little cloudy. Colors ran together as though water was being poured over them. Individual colors gathered into big patches, which was at least fairly interesting to look at. Monet must have suffered from the same condition. I had no sense of contrast and no depth perception. I had no peripheral vision either. The worst part was at dusk, when

I was practically blind. Though it was the same in strong sunlight, winter or summer. After a while, my condition stabilized. I was prepared to make the best of it. That's just the way it was . . . I strained to see. I squinted. I used magnifying glasses. I bought some eyeglasses that were the size of dinner plates, but the only thing they gave me was a headache. Finally I developed cataracts, and then everything disappeared entirely, the pastel colors too. But losing my sight wasn't the worst of it. I can't even remember ever seeing anything especially beautiful, back when I could still see. No, the worst was the dried-up ice-cold old bitch responsible for making me aware of my condition. She sat quite calmly with her legs crossed and told me about what, in all likelihood, would happen to me, sooner or later. And she was exactly right. It seemed logical, afterward, to blame her . . .

I'd thought that I should get a driver's license and so had to submit to a physical examination. The old bitch was the doctor who was assigned to examine me; she fastened some clamps onto my eyelids, both upper and lower. They were like the tiny claws of some tiny bird of prey. Next, she put some blue-colored fluid in my eyes, which gave me the irresistible urge to blink, something that her little contraptions were intended to prevent . . .

After a while, she got around to examining me with her own magnifying glass. I heard a "Sweet Jesus!" slip out of her. She led me to understand that there would be no driver's license. It wasn't even open to discussion. Not only that, but I had to wear a patch over one eye for two days after this to confirm what the old bitch had already made crystal clear, that things were going to get really bad in a relatively short time . . . I began to live in a constant night, though even now the dark isn't total. I am, so to speak, not quite there yet. I choose to look at this as a transitional phase. It's best to sit quietly, leaning back, and close my eyes at regular intervals, nap and wake up, nap and wake up, according to a pattern, more or less, and simply accept that the world is

gray, increasingly gray, gray to such an extent that I've forgotten
how real colors used to look. I heard someone mention red on
the radio or TV, and the green of the grass, and felt like I was
being insulted . . .
Certainly I'd lost something when my sight was reduced to this
approximate blindness. But I was also liberated, in a way. I didn't
have to see anything ugly or abominable anymore. I stopped
having to wonder whether I was seeing this or that correctly or
not. Regardless, I got a kick out of the doctor's description of
my condition, yes, approximate blindness, even though I can't
be sure if he coined the term out of consideration for my feelings
or for the convenience of my insurance company . . .
I am approximately blind, I said to myself. So, there is something,
a place, a small opening in this putrid darkness, a tiny ray of light,
if I can only look long enough to find it. In other words, things
weren't completely hopeless . . . anyway, I like to sit like this and
nod off because when I sleep, I dream, and then I'm able to see.
Then I see everything just like I used to. Then, everything is in
place again in front of me just like I remember it. But every time
I wake up again, I lose my sight. Then it becomes night. The
eternal gray darkness surrounds me like a tight-fitting shroud;
tight, but, nevertheless, limitless . . .
Sweetie thinks I'm abominable. She can hardly bear to look at
me. She holds her breath when she has to come in here. I can hear
it. She pants like a dog. It's a wonder she manages to change me
without throwing up. This body is a sewer. A sewer is all that's
left of it. I'm well aware of my situation. It's all right under my
nose, after all. My stinking scraps. Is it really so strange that it's
difficult for me to focus on my thoughts? Is it really so strange
that I can't taste my food? If they open me up after I've said
farewell to them all, all my pent-up sewage will waft out of me,
everything at once, leaving nothing but a reeking pile of skin.
That will be my revenge. I'll poison them from beyond. The

so-called experts. They'll get it right in their faces. Everything
I've taken in and carried with me all these years: all my sorrows,
all my confusion, everything I've had to hold in again and again.
Sometimes I've been so miserable that I've felt it all blowing me
up like a balloon . . .
"What happened to the man I married?" Sweetie asks herself.
Where is he? And who's this, this monster that's taken his place?
Who's that sitting in his chair? Who's that pissing in his catheter?
Who's that sitting there with his mouth hanging open? It's only
a matter of time before the door gets knocked down and a big
machine rolls in to get me, I'm sure of it, lifts me out of my chair
with its pincers, and tosses me into the back of a truck like a limp
sack of shit . . . And meanwhile, out in the kitchen, Sweetie is signing
the papers, thanking the nice men for coming so quickly . . .
Yes, they're probably on their way. I try to get information out
of her, but I'm no wiser than if I'd tried to have a conversation
with her asshole. I've asked her to tell me how my eyes look, but
she won't say a thing. She talks around the subject in such a way
that I'm certain she thinks they're unpleasant to look at. There's
not much I can do about that. I move them from one side to the
other, but I can't tell the difference. Nothing changes. It doesn't
get any lighter for me, and it doesn't get any darker. I roll my
eyes around, swinging them to all points, until I almost puke. I
stare. I let my gaze fall on different places in the room, and then
I try to guess what I'm actually looking at. The sink, the toilet,
the window, the bathtub, the towel rack, the mirror . . .
I imagine that anyone who had to spend any time here in the
bathroom with me, Sigri for instance, if she had to pee so
badly someday that she had no other choice than to come in,
yes, I imagine that if I stared right at her, she would find the
experience singularly uncomfortable, and that it wouldn't do her
a bit of good to remind herself that I couldn't actually see her.
She would break out in a cold sweat if I stared at her too long,

she'd be terrified of my pair of dead eyes, yes, a living gaze could never make her feel such a suffocating fear. She would lick my feet if I asked her. And I should . . . yes, I would be well within my rights to do all this . . . I could turn this bathroom into a living hell for her in the time it takes her to pee or shit and wash her hands afterwards. Oh, yes . . .

Yes, our little maid feels sick at the mere thought of dealing with me, the sickness comes on when she imagines my watery eyes looking right through her. She doesn't know what to do, she breaks out in a cold sweat, claws at herself in confusion. I could drive her out of her mind if I wanted to, send her screaming down into the abyss, make her so miserable that she'd finally be willing to do just about anything in order to end the nightmare . . .

It's my world in here. Here, my word is law. I know this room like the back of my hand. It's as though I have a map of the room in my mind, and I'm intimately familiar with all its sounds, I hear even the slightest movement . . . That hollow sound when Sweetie pushes past the bathtub . . . And that deep gurgle, as though from someplace beneath the earth, when she wriggles around on the toilet to get comfortable . . . when she gets those tiny wrinkles at her temples, sitting, squinting too hard . . . It's true, nothing that anyone does in here escapes my attention. I need to know their positions and what they're doing at every moment. And whenever anyone else is here, anyone aside from Sweetie, that is, I immediately have the upper hand, immediately score a decisive victory over nature, over what nature's taken away from me, now wholly at ease, empowered. It's me who dominates the situation. I'm like God, who also has dead eyes, a gaze that rests on us but sees nothing, and which we know sees nothing, but to which we all subordinate ourselves nonetheless, whenever we think it might be turned our way . . .

Sigri is in the apartment, oh yes, I hear her, her voice is unmistakable, cluck cluck cluck, now they're cackling like hens out there, they'll be gossiping for hours, you'd think they were the same age, just as old as each other, or maybe just as young . . . Why did she volunteer to start doing our shopping for us? What was her ulterior motive? I managed at the last moment to prevent Sweetie from giving her a key, so she could let herself in. I shudder to think how many copies would be floating around out there now if I hadn't. The house would be swarming with people. Like an anthill. Sweetie wouldn't be able to open a door without knocking someone over . . . one of those small, dishonest creatures, prone to stealing, who populate the world. If only Sweetie would bring her in here one day, then I'd have a chance to hear what her voice really sounds like. She could come in and sing a song. I hardly know a thing about her, even though she's in the apartment almost every single week . . .

If she'd only come in here once a week and empty her bowels . . . if I only could get to know another smell besides Erna's, if I could take in the scent of a fresh, youthful bowel movement, right here in my bathroom . . . it would help me through my days, that scent, carrying me along on its light, airy arms . . . I would ask her not to flush . . . I'd be in paradise for hours. I would sit with my head in a fragrant cloud, alone with my thoughts . . .

And yet, how can I be certain there's really such a person as Sigri? A helpful little bitch, I hear. I've never seen her. I've barely even heard her. How can I be sure it's really her, or that she's called Sigri, or that it's the same person who comes by each time, or what she's really doing here? I only have Sweetie's word to go on, and that woman, well, she twists everything around to suit herself, for all I know she's letting them all live here, the people who do the housework for her, she could have a houseful of employees here without my knowing anything about it, all sitting out there silent as muses, making eyes at each other . . .

I'm not allowed to know much of anything that goes on here, I don't count, they don't think I'm important, Sweetie stopped consulting me about things a long time ago, she barely even considers me among the living, I'm just a thing to her, an object, I sit in her bathroom and take up space. Why doesn't she get anyone to come and move me? She knows that she can do whatever she wants with me, she certainly knows I'm helpless, she doesn't need to show me the least consideration, after all, so what's the problem, is she afraid? Afraid of what I might say? How I might take it? That would be a new one, she's always put everyone else's feelings ahead of mine, never lifting a finger to shelter me, leaving me right in the middle of things, so I just sit where she puts me, what else can I do, if I'm in her way she should just move me, why doesn't she move me if I'm in the way, why doesn't she just stick me in a corner? Why don't you move me, you goddamned bitch, what are you afraid of? Move me so there'll finally be some room for you in here!

A quiet life. I can't get away from it. Whether or not it's actually in my power to get away makes no difference to me. As far as I'm concerned, I move an arm, turn my head, lift one leg and cross it over the other, and that's about it, there's not much more I can do. Then I swallow a meatball or two to calm my stomach, take some pills, and drift off . . . It's the same thing every day, I open my eyes, take a breath, wet my lips, chew the dryness out of my mouth, clear my throat, get my voice back, shout at Sweetie. Old Amonsen was right when he said that it all comes down to the heart, now . . . I've got nothing left to say in this life, but my heart, it almost scares me, it just keeps beating and beating, like it'll never stop. I take a diuretic, which makes me extra tired, dizzy too, depending on how much I've eaten. Which is not to say my mood is particularly good even when I don't take one . . . I'd sure love to have something for the dizziness, but Doctor Amonsen said that it would be risky to take both medications at the same time . . .

Which is nothing but a load of shit, there's no risk at all, the only people who risk anything are the young and healthy, otherwise there's nothing to lose . . . My body is so full of bacteria and other tiny creatures, I can't see that I'm in any danger at all . . . It's them that have something to fear, not me . . . I'm nothing but a buffet to them, they eat and breed and one beautiful day they'll have me by the throat, my body will be all bacteria all the way up to my throat. It's them who eat the meatballs that Sweetie makes, not me . . . that's why they're here, to get fed, and that's the only reason I have to eat. If they weren't around, I'd probably get along fine with just the occasional drink . . . so I swallow small pieces of food for my tiny creatures, to give them something to munch on. I'm not myself, no, I'm so full of filth that it's doubtful whether it's actually me who's sitting here, no, it's not me, it's all them, the others, they're what's holding me up, they've eaten through everything, this body consists of bacteria from the chin down, they're inside me and I'm inside them, every single one of them, I'm made up of thousands of little units, each of which have a thin carapace, a pair of tiny eyes, and some minuscule legs, in fact, they're just teeming with legs, and the legs never stop moving, I'm just the host, I lift my arm, I turn my head, but it's not me doing it, it's them . . .

The worms peek out of my nose, and they fall out when they get too long. Some time ago, Sweetie tried to pull them out for me. She nagged and nagged to get me to let her do it . . . I itch. That's why I try not to move. I know what I look like . . . I'm full of sores, or tiny little holes, one here, one there, so even though I can't manage to actually touch anything, to feel anything, I have to scratch, I just scratch, I scratch in places where I haven't felt any real sensations for centuries, phantom pains are what they call it, that's some name . . . Where are my girls? If they were around, they would have come with tweezers and cotton balls and cleaned me, taken away the worms, they were so talented, they did everything so well, no matter how small or meaningless the task, yes, they would master it. But they're not around. They don't even know that I'm sitting here. They've forgotten me, most of them, perhaps all of them . . . maybe there isn't a single soul left up there who remembers that they once had a director named Edwin Mortens and that he did an absolutely impeccable job, really cleaned up the place, impeccable . . . maybe no one will remember his name until many years from now, when my worms are sleeping satiated in the grass, and a young doctor pulls a pair of our old account books down from the shelves, filling the air with dust, and then more dust, a cloud, as he begins to blow it off them . . .

Miserable, miserable me . . . all my life I've taken care of other people, but now there's no one to take care of me . . .

It isn't even worth asking Sweetie, not lately, it's all she can do to scratch my ear, if I beg her. She tosses her meatballs up into my lap without saying anything . . .

The worms are twisting around down inside me. And the dead . . . they're impatient, waiting for me, pushing and shoving each other around, trying to make room for one more. But I have one advantage that they didn't, when they first got there. I'm used to the dark. Someone closed my eyes long ago, so I'd be prepared for what's coming . . .

No, no, no, I shouldn't think any more about death now, the doctor said that I think entirely too much about death, it'll come when it comes, he said, as if that did me any good. I think about death all the time, I can't manage to leave it alone, it's like having a plastic tube down your throat, you can't swallow without feeling it . . .

But you have to draw the line somewhere. It's better to pull the plug than live like that, strapped down, with those inexplicable contraptions sticking out of both ends, Christ, what's the point of letting a machine keep you alive when your own machinery is all worn out? I'll manage to stick around as long as I have Sweetie; the day she falls, it'll be the end for me too . . .

Of course, she hopes I go first, then she'd have a few quiet years to herself, and far be it from me to say that she doesn't deserve it after the way she's looked after me all of these years. That's what spouses do for each other, without ever asking for something in return . . . She has only two arms and two legs, for Christ's sake, even though there have been times she could have used four or five of each. Sure, she'll breathe a real sigh of relief when I've taken my last breath . . .

I don't have anything against letting her have a couple of years to herself, why not, as a well-deserved reward. In a fit of sentimentality, or I don't know what, I offered that horny super of ours fifty thousand in cash, all at once, if he would take some tool or other out of his bag and beat my head in with it. The idiot didn't even do me the courtesy of a response. He thought that I was sitting here and talking shit, leading him on . . .

Still, the truth is that it was smart of him to refuse me. He saw how unreasonable the request was. A sharp young man. That much was clear. He knows when to be careful. Where in the world would I find fifty thousand in cash anyway? No, it wouldn't be the smart thing, to kill me, when he couldn't be sure of getting his money. Would have been a different story if I'd been sitting here with cash in hand. He knew what was what. Only an idiot wouldn't insist on payment in advance on a job like that . . .

Oh, yes. I know his type. Afterwards, he sat out in my living room and smoked a cigarette. It wasn't possible to breathe in here. He sat and puffed away out there like he owned the place. What could Sweetie be thinking, letting guys like that into the apartment and asking them to make themselves at home? Coffee, finger cakes, maybe a nip of something stronger, well, I guess I don't have anything against it, at heart, he's young, he can't help himself, and she's old, she needs a little distraction from time to time . . .

He's young, yes, he can do whatever the hell he wants, can get away with anything, things have changed, the world isn't like it was, in the old days you had to specialize, you had to pick one thing and then they made damn sure you stuck to it, but you, you horny bastard, sure, you can pass yourself off as an expert in whatever area happens to take your fancy, just have a quick look in a book on the subject five minutes before you show up for work, and presto, you're a specialist, a plumber one day, a gardener the next, and then off to convert some heathens come the weekend, should the need arise . . .

It's not always the best who last the longest. That was something De-Sarg told me once. I don't know why I'm thinking of that now. And I'm not even sure I know what he meant, exactly, when he said it . . .

The only thing left to do is keep my mind active. Until it's all over. If things come to a dead stop up there, like they have everywhere else, then I'm finished. But it's a nightmare, keeping my thoughts straight. I've got to be careful. Sometimes, I forget things I ought to remember. Careless. It's like the things I know I should say to Sweetie the next time she comes in here have all dried up and blown away by the time she actually comes . . .

Today, I fell asleep with chewing gum in my mouth. I've never done that before. When I woke up and opened my mouth, it was like I had a lump of concrete wedged between my teeth . . .

"IT. SMELLS. LIKE. Smoke." That was the first thing he said when I opened the door. I had to push it open with my elbow since I was carrying both a plate and a mug. He was sitting with his head bowed over his lap. His beard moved gently. It was as though he had to reposition the huge wad of chewing gum in his mouth between each word in order to find enough room for what he wanted to say.

"Was it. You. Smoking?" he asked, though he knew perfectly well it wasn't me. I didn't answer. I wasn't in any mood, all of a sudden, to deal with him. "Or was it. That young guy? I thought. Didn't he. Leave?"

I didn't say anything. I didn't need to say anything. He'd waited so long for me to come that he didn't have time to listen to me anyway. He started off with how inconsiderate it had been of me to let a stranger into the house, and a young person at that. You never knew what you could expect from someone like that, no matter what kind of job he had. Behind even the most exemplary façade, he proclaimed, there hides a greedy wolf cub. He asked whether I'd checked if anything had been stolen. I told him he could relax. The super had been a good boy. He was also quite handy. I had no complaints. But Edwin wouldn't let

up. He said handiness was the perfect disguise. He claimed he'd
heard the super open the medicine cabinet and root around after
he'd finished changing the bulb. Edwin insisted I go and check
if anything was missing. I asked him to think carefully before he
started making accusations against people he barely knew. But
he continued his tirade: "That crook!" he screamed. "I know his
kind!" His jaw moved up and down like it was possessed. I'm sure
he chews gum specifically to make it hard for me to understand
what he's saying—not that it really matters what he's saying when
he gets like this. What was strange, what I was noticing for the
first time now, was how much sharper the light had become in
the bathroom. Everything was so much clearer. Maybe that was
why the super's work had seemed so impressive. Edwin looked
paler than ever. His arms were like marzipan. The super must
have used a higher-wattage fluorescent bulb than the one we had
before. I guess it'll use more electricity too, especially with the
lights on day and night. It makes no difference to Edwin, but it
certainly does to me. It reminded me of the lights in a hospital
more than anything else. I went and peeked in the mirror. The
light made my face look as though it was covered in red blotches.

I didn't know what to say. I stood there and tried to look
at Edwin with the young man's eyes. I tried to imagine what it
must have been like for the super to come in here and see Edwin
sitting there when he wasn't used to that kind of thing, probably
not used to old people at all. Or maybe he was, since he was the
super, and probably was always going around helping the older
residents with every little problem. They probably asked him to
do all sorts of inconsequential things. So, maybe Edwin wasn't
that terrible a sight for the super after all, in his huge slippers,
shiny jogging suit, and the shirt I sewed for him, which I took a
lot of trouble to do right. It turned out so nicely that the seams
weren't visible. I couldn't see them myself, even if I tried. For
all I knew, the super had thought that I was the disgusting one,

not Edwin. Maybe it was my life, not Edwin's, that had been so confusing for him to contemplate, sitting there with me in the living room. Once upon a time, I used to clip Edwin's nails, both fingers and toes. I even managed to push back his cuticles, if I didn't have anything else to attend to. I trimmed his beard and tweezed his nose hairs—they were stiff and hard, I remember, totally unlike all the other hair on his body. His nose hair looked inhuman. I also squeezed the blackheads out of his nose. Cleaned his ears. I trimmed the dead skin off his heels. I washed and combed his hair—every day. I insisted that he look presentable, even though no one, more or less, ever set eyes on him—even though he sat there alone all the time. I even pressed on his stomach to help him get the air out. Maybe our young super would have seen everything in a different light and felt great sympathy for Edwin if he'd met him then, when he still got up once in a while, still walked around, still resembled a man, a gentleman, a human being. And when there wasn't so much garbage in there. The entire bathroom floor is almost covered in foil gum wrappers and empty paper packaging. It's like a flower garden. The mess stretches all the way over to the corner with the bathtub. Edwin's chest of drawers sticks up from the sea of trash like a cliff, and on top of it are unopened packages of gum in neat little stacks, arranged according to color, according to his precise instructions. He only needs to reach his arm out to get them. Maybe Edwin and the super had a little chat. Maybe they felt a mutual sympathy. Maybe they came to a kind of understanding. Maybe the young man would start to drop by from time to time in order to continue their chat. Edwin certainly had a lot of interesting things to say to someone who would take the time to listen, someone he felt a connection to, someone he wanted to impress. He loved to tell stories. He's read books about famous people, travelogues that go on for hundreds of pages. He used to tell the best stories to me over and over again—even better, I think, than the ones who

had written them to begin with. He also couldn't keep himself
from telling me all about the remarkable things that were always
happening at Kronsæther—though he always used to add that
he wasn't really supposed to discuss those things, not ever, that
he didn't really have permission to tell a particular story. But
then he told it anyway—but only after he got me to swear that
I would never repeat it to another soul. Who could I have told?
But I always thought those stories about the old people were hilarious—even though I knew Edwin was exaggerating everything
to make them seem more hopeless and comical than they actually
were. I remember there was one of them who thought his legs
were only something you used when you were sitting down, so
couldn't understand why they always went with him whenever
he stood up again! But I never thought we were being cruel to those
people, even though we were laughing at them. Edwin didn't either,
absolutely not. I think it was a way for him to learn to accept
them, to endure their perpetual complaints and suffering. Edwin
always used to talk about death as though a person could decide
for himself whether or not to be conscious of it. For him, it was
first and foremost a question of having the right attitude—if I
understood him correctly. It didn't really seem like he understood
how relevant this was to his own work situation—that his job
was to oversee the process of death. No, he applied the same
standards to everyone, in Kronsæther or out in the world. And
he always told me when someone at Kronsæther had passed on.
Sometimes I knew them by name, sometimes not, but he kept
strict accounts, always balancing the books of the living and the
dead. I was his secretary. I took down the information for every
single one. I liked to listen to him. It was as though the people
he talked about were real and unreal at the same time. I didn't
know them. I never saw them. But I knew that they existed, or
had until a few days ago, or a few hours ago. They were distant
enough that I felt I could allow myself to dwell on the worst

without it wearing me down—everything that Edwin told me was so tragic, or hilarious, or both, that thinking about the most terrible parts of these people's lives became a comfort to me. And it often happened that I couldn't let them go after a story was over—that I found myself developing a deep and abiding interest and sympathy for all his characters, one after the other. And Edwin never seemed to run out of stories. It was as though he had an entire little world at his fingertips—an endless well to draw from.

Before he lost his sight, he was always so meticulous with whatever he did. He planned everything down to the smallest detail, thought everything out beforehand, considered every possible repercussion before setting a plan in motion. He drew up diagrams for the smallest tasks, covering pages with tiny figures, arrows, and letters, as though he expected strangers to carry out his instructions long-distance. It was almost ridiculous, this painful exactitude. He would take hours to refine something that could have been done in a couple of seconds. It was as though he couldn't bear to see the results of his actions if he hadn't taken an unbelievably long time to work something out in advance. But I've never seen such beautiful handwriting. Each stroke was like a wave crossing the paper. He wrote with an old fountain pen, always with the same pen. He didn't want to look at anything else, not even a pencil. It was the split nub of his pen that made his writing particularly harmonious, he explained to me. It created a balance between thick and thin strokes. He made a special face whenever he wrote—I called it his "concentration face"—it looked like he was going to sneeze . . . In a strange way, I felt that his painfully exacting nature was his way of showing some kind of concern for . . . I don't know . . . It was as if Edwin, always so meticulous, put himself through all that in order to demonstrate that he was able to take care of me . . . as though he was telling me, via his constant planning, his endless accumulation of little details, that I didn't need to be afraid. I don't know if it ever occurred to him to think that that was what he was doing, but I think it's true. He'd built a wall around me, to defend me—that was how I came to see it . . . Though the wall certainly got on my nerves. I felt compelled to break out of it, to destroy everything he'd built up, but there was something about his conviction—his blind faith—that held me back. I couldn't do it, not because I was worried about what would happen to me, but out of consideration for him.

The only thing he was afraid of—on the subject of getting older—was that he would lose his mind. If his heart kept on working the same as it always had, he decided, the rest should too. He took a test once to see how high his IQ was. I don't remember his score, but he must have mentioned it, which means that he must have been pleased. They'd seen he had a good head on his shoulders, he said. He always did a number of calculations in his head during his meetings with the management, and, as a rule, he always came up with the answer long before the others did—and they were using calculators. And never, never—according to him—did he give them a wrong answer. If there were discrepancies, the people with calculators simply redid their figures, until it all came out right. So Edwin made me promise to kill him if he ever started going senile. I had to swear on my mother's grave that I would do everything in my power to take his life the day he started seeming like he . . . how did he put it? He had a little stock of different expressions that he liked to use: like he'd *gone 'round the bend, coo-coo, had a screw loose.* I can't remember all of them. I thought they all sounded a bit childish coming out of a grown man's mouth. I never was able to decide whether he actually meant all that, or if it was just talk. In any case, it was pretty hard to take him seriously when he looked me in the eyes, his face pale and mournful, and said *coo-coo.* At the same time, however, I couldn't help but see that there was a dreadful seriousness behind his words—even if they were spoken in jest—a terrifying gravity. His tone of voice gave me the shivers, even when it was clear he was making a joke, even when he laughed—because he did—about his demands. He wanted me to kill him. He asked and he asked. On the day he was no longer himself, Edwin wanted me to help him end everything—on the day he went 'round the bend. He never recanted. Never said anything to make me think he'd had a change of heart. That's what he feared the most, a protracted, idiotic old age—I couldn't stand seeing him that way, and he wouldn't stand the thought of it, but if he did lose his mind, it would almost be a blessing: he wouldn't understand what had happened to him, and wouldn't understand what I was about to do. In any case, he also made me solely responsible for deciding whether or not he'd lost his mind, whether or not he'd reached the point where he was no longer himself—but how can you really know something like that, if a person has a *screw loose* . . . maybe they're only going through some kind of passing phase, a temporary mental disturbance, something that looks like senility but isn't? I tried to take his request seriously, but everything seemed more unreal and grotesque the more I thought about it, and these anxieties cast a shadow over my thoughts for the future. I couldn't talk to anyone about it either. They'd just think we were both crazy. Imagine, a husband exacting that kind of promise from his wife, with the intention that she honor it for the rest of their lives! That it be taken as holy writ the day the worst comes to pass, the day you've lived in dread of for years and years! What did he know about getting old? He was still young. And I tortured myself thinking over the various ways to carry out my promise, trying to choose the best. I imagined myself standing over him, shaking, with a knife in my hand. I imagined myself coming at him from behind with a towel wound around my hands . . .

Now, however, his mind is all he has left. He protects it like a priceless antique. It's like his head contains a huge archive. He sits in there and leafs through old folders, day in and day out, for fear of forgetting. I hardly remember anything now, except the things that made the most impression on me. Whereas it seems like Edwin's forgotten all the important things in favor of retaining mounds of insignificant trivia. He has such a good mind. Why does he waste it on such inconsequential things? He's so incredibly picky—he's always been like that—that there just isn't any room in him for other, deeper feelings. There's only space for the small and the worthless. What's more, his memory is superhuman. Every detail is recorded. Even facets of the most insignificant event. Maybe if he'd put his memory to better use, he'd value forgetting a little more. But I don't contradict him. He's the one at the center of our little reality. It's Edwin who's at the controls, piloting me here and there all day, now into the pantry to get a new bottle of something for him . . . now over to the stove to put a pan of something on the fire . . . over to the refrigerator to get a can of cola . . . Anyway, he just sits there, sits there in that heirloom of his, which he insists would have brought in thousands of crowns if he'd ever wanted to sell it. A wheelchair was out of the question. It was the rocking chair or we could bury him there and then and be finished with the whole thing. That's what he said on the day they were here with the machine and lifted him into it. He's just not interested in anything aside from what goes on in his head. If I didn't know better, I'd think he was praying. That he was talking to God. He's like a monk who's forsaken the world, who sees it and its people as a distraction. But he isn't praying. He's just tormenting himself. It seems like that's the only thing he's capable of doing. Again and again, he goes through the list of things that bother him most. I don't know what's on that list, and I don't want to know either. He can keep his pain and suffering to himself. He complains all the time—sometimes I feel like his mouth is connected to the bathroom doorknob, as if I activate it whenever I happen to walk in—telling me how bad a caretaker I am, how badly I treat him, how careless I am, how little consideration I show him, how much better it would be if we had a professional nurse, yes, a young one, he says, in a white uniform, with plenty of time on her hands, and big tits . . . And if I go to answer the telephone, he's calling out again as soon as I turn my back on the bathroom, demanding to know who called, who I'm fooling around with, whether I'm thinking about running away and leaving him in a lurch, helpless as he is, or as he insists he is. But he's not, really . . . never has been. I've never known anyone as self-sufficient as Edwin. He just sits there, just like that, day or night, thinking. It's the only thing he does. He's like a big spider, sitting there and spinning his web, using all these years to cover everything with the fine mesh net of his thoughts. I always have to be careful where I step. He's never stopped spinning his web, and I never noticed how much I'd become caught in it. It's like none of this will ever end. His lungs are full of cartilage. Only one of them still seems to work. I think that's why he has problems swallowing. A nasty cold would be enough to finish him off. That's what Dr. Amonsen said. I think about it everyday. When he gets quiet, it's like an alarm. I can't help it. If the bathroom goes quiet, I become nervous. I start to think it's already happened. Then I hear his voice, first softly, then louder and louder, until he's screaming at the top of his lungs, almost like he's somehow heard what I was thinking, and wants to announce, in triumph, that he's still here, that he's alive and awake. I don't know. He uses his right shoulder as a pillow, always the right. So often that there's a shoulder-shaped depression in his cheek.

In the beginning, he had a radio. He left it on around the clock. I hated going into the bathroom in the morning. It sounded like it was full of people. But then I read an article in the paper that reminded me of how dangerous it could be to have a radio in there, considering how much water was around. Besides, the shows he listened to just upset him; he believed everything he heard—blindly, as it were. There wasn't a day he didn't get some new and grand idea because of the thing, and of course it was vitally important for him to convince me that action had to be taken immediately. Once he grabbed me and demanded that I get a dentist to come over to replace his old fillings with gold ones! He said that that's why he always had so many headaches, because of the amalgam fillings in his teeth. I asked him if he realized how much this would cost. He said it made no difference, the only thing that mattered was that he wouldn't have those terrible pains in his mouth and head anymore. I didn't need to ask where this idea had come from. I tried my best to bring him back to earth. I told him that we were looking at a scenario in which he would presumably have to pay tens of thousands of crowns for something that he'd completely forget about a couple of years later. But he wouldn't give up. He wanted gold fillings. With porcelain crowns. There was no budging him. I don't listen to the radio myself. I've tried, but when I do, I just feel like I'm listening to him the whole time—as though his voice is there, in the background, almost drowned out by the static, but not quite—whether it's music or a talk show, every single sound caries his voice. I hear him screaming out for his life. I can't manage to follow what he's saying, exactly. I just sit and listen. I'm never sure whether it's really him or not. The best thing for someone like me, who can't hear so well, is to live in complete silence. That way, if something's really happening, something serious, I can hear it immediately. But maybe I should have let him keep the radio. Maybe one of those small ones, that run on batteries. Completely safe. With earplugs. That would give him something else besides his own thoughts to concentrate on, in whatever time is left to him. Right now, he doesn't even have anything to measure this time with. He doesn't know how long a day is, doesn't know how long he's been sitting in there, how many years it's been. If it wasn't for me, he would never be able to keep track of time. He can't tell the difference between falling asleep for five minutes and falling asleep for five hours. It's all the same to him, once he wakes up.

WELL, HERE SHE comes, my prison warden, shuffle, shuffle . . . Whenever she opens the door, a slight breeze flows over my face, and it makes the gum wrappers on the floor rustle . . . Isn't she coming? I thought she was on her way. She should have been here a while ago . . .

I've meant to talk to her about getting some help here at home, someone could come in a couple of days a week to look after me, then Sweetie could get some rest, since right now it all falls to her, and she isn't as young as she used to be, but I'm afraid we won't get anywhere if she calls a service and asks, she'd make the whole situation come off badly, make it sound strange, and they'd just refuse, they'd turn her away, and of course she'd just give up, she doesn't dare contradict anyone, but honestly, if there's someone who desperately needs help, it's me . . . That's why it's so important that she takes the right tack when approaching them, that's why I'll have to explain to her exactly what she needs to say to them, word for word . . . I wish she would get in here before I forget it all . . .

No . . .

She waltzed right by, what's she doing out there anyway, out among the colors, is she trying to drive me insane? I'm sitting here

absolutely burning with all the things I have to tell her, but she
stays away despite the fact that she knows there are things I want
to tell her, she has no problem just puttering aimlessly around the
apartment for hours on end without having anything in particular
to do. She's avoiding me, avoiding coming in here, I'm sure that
she's pissing in the kitchen sink just to avoid coming in here . . .
She's a terrible procrastinator, days for her are divided up into
hours and hours divided up into minutes, oh there's always plenty
of time for her to get around to something, but for me, for me
every day is nothing more than a putrid darkness. Time stands
still, time smells like shit just like everything else in here smells
like shit, it's almost as though the odor is actually coming out of
my own nose . . .
. . . The window in front of me might as well be a wall. I know
that there's a plastic curtain hanging in front of it decorated with
a picture of a fortress, an elegant path, and a crowd of pleasure
boats in sparkling water, but I have no idea whether the curtain
is open or closed . . .
I should have a clock in here so I can keep track of the minutes
and seconds . . .
Idiot! Then you'd just have to work out the time whenever you
wake up . . .
I used to love to note the time of day, I used to make a note of
the time of day whenever I could, the pages of my desk calendar
were full of these notes, it was a special joy for me, I don't know
why, to write down the hour and the minutes with a heavy line
underneath, and then to see it standing there like something
irrefutable, something it was impossible to doubt, something
it was impossible to avoid. The perfect time of day, the most
harmonious of all times, was six o'clock in the evening, eighteen
hundred hours . . . I would always suggest we have a management
meeting at that particular time just to allow myself the joy of
writing "6:00," first in my desk calendar, then my daily planner,

and finally on the weekly schedule hanging on the wall in the meeting room.

I'm neither desperate nor especially patient, and I realize that this is a problem for me. The result is that my life has developed at an exceedingly slow pace, almost imperceptibly. I've lived a life that it hasn't always been easy to stay interested in. So, I don't have anything especially wonderful to look back on. It's like the whole thing only took a couple of hours . . .

I am not curious. I don't give a damn what other people do. Why the hell should I bother knowing anything about them when they don't know anything about me? There isn't anyone besides Sweetie who knows what my situation is. No, not even her. She thinks she does, but she doesn't. God only knows what she's telling other people about me . . .

I despise them . . . car, boat, house, job, two arms, two legs, happy children, they don't know anything about what it means to live, they have no idea what a simple thought can develop into, they don't know anything about thought and they don't know what it's like to sit in a chair day after day and bear the weight of a half-dead body and a head that's far too big . . .

The consumer price index has risen more than six percent . . . that was the last thing I heard before Sweetie came and took the radio away and said she'd read somewhere that there was a serious danger she could get roasted alive if the radio fell into the bathtub with her. The consumer price index has risen more than six percent. That was all I thought about for days. There wasn't room for any other sentences in my mind, only that one, even if it was a load of shit . . .

There's little in my memory to cheer me up, a lot that I would have been happy to forget, but I've never had the luxury of forgetting anything, the moment I think of something, I know it'll follow me to the grave . . .

All things considered, I was glad when she came and took the radio away, it was getting on my nerves, the reception was terrible, the antenna picked up every damn thing, every time the thermostat out there clicked on or off, the speakers started crackling, it was awful, like the people in the radio studio had started farting into the microphones . . .

It's never completely quiet, never, not for ears like mine. I hear everything there is to hear and even a bit more, I hear things buzz inside my head, it happens whether it's day or night, like someone's left a machine running . . .

I'm no thinker, but I think all the time. It's the only thing I can't stop doing. Completely natural, but unbearable nevertheless. Every thought raises another, and they all resemble one another, so that each ugly child bears the mark of its forefathers.

It's a nightmare. It's like a never-ending surgical operation . . . it's like waking up from sedation right in the middle of an operation . . . I lift my head, I look down on myself, and there's my entire inner life sitting on a plate right next to me, prepared like some exotic meal, but I have no appetite for it . . .

Will I never get any rest? Is there any rest to be had? Is this curse really endless? I have to try to think of something else . . . I have to do my best, maybe think about something erotic, I always find my way back to that subject, something really vulgar, something to help pass the time, I try as hard as I can, using all my concentration, but unfortunately I can't manage it, I guess I've burned myself out . . .

Where is this road heading? What will become of everything? Will the future be like what's already going on in my head? No, the world's still out there. Nothing ever goes away, it just accumulates. Especially for me, who can't see worth a damn, yes, I just sit here with a head full of stupid pictures . . .

I need to contract a serious illness, one that could keep me busy with some new pains, occupy me with a merciless attack on my body and soul. An illness would give me perspective on things.

It would give me something else to think about, something that might be able to clear out all the junk cluttering up my head, most of it absolutely awful, and allow me to reach a higher plane. If I had a serious illness, I'd have something to keep track of time with. If I had a serious illness, I'd be able to look forward to it developing, I'd have some kind of future to look forward to. But I don't. My future is dark, just a single, eternal, putrid darkness. I have nothing to hold on to, I have nothing to connect myself to, nothing to look forward to, nothing to help keep track of the time that passes alongside all my nothing . . .

Heart attacks . . . Pneumonia . . . Emphysema . . . they had everything you could think of, up at Kronsæther, even a case of syphilis, but this wasn't really talked about out loud . . . there was so much to die from that it was often impossible to tell which disease had had the last word. They gurgled and gasped as we held them, with a hundred different evil spirits in their bodies . . . I remember Mr. Wilhelmsen, with that stomach of his, left the world with a gasp that could only be described as lascivious, so much so you'd have thought he finally got his way with one of the nurses. He left behind an utter chaos of possible explanations for his demise. The doctor who came to examine him just shook his head. Anyway, Wilhelmsen was so full of morphine there at the end that he could've just died of an overdose, for all I know . . . It didn't matter, everyone was just happy to be rid of him, both his family and his roommates. His breath had smelled like paraffin, and he used to spend every night lying in bed calling out the names of all the women he'd known . . .

Cancer, that's what I'd like most, a real illness, a disease that stinks of death right off the bat. I'd love a pernicious little tumor somewhere in my system, somewhere it could do the most possible damage, in my throat, or colon, or wherever, maybe in the intestines, or down in my lungs, sure, I could treat the tumor like a pet dog or cat. It would get everything it needed. And no

one would be allowed to hurt it. I'd defend it tooth and nail . . .
I've always wanted a tube up my nose, it would make everything
seem more real, all the bits of you that are falling apart . . .
That's why no one remembers me, because I'm not sick. That's
why no one knows I'm still alive, that I'm still sitting here, breathing in and out just like everyone else. If I'd actually become
sick, though, they'd all know, word would have spread in a hurry,
and they'd all be talking about me, news would've spread all at
once, someone would have mentioned me and asked some
other someone if they'd heard anything more about how I was
getting along, then maybe some of them would have come to
visit, they would've been worried, they would have been curious
to know everything they could find out about how I was doing,
whether I was holding on. But I'm not sick. So no one talks about
me. I'm nowhere. No one knows whether I'm alive or dead . . .
If you're ill, you should be seriously ill. If you get old, you should
get really really old, then drop dead after a couple of days. De-
Sarg's face went completely gray. A rare liver condition. He talked
about it like you talk about dead heroes from back in the war.
Whenever he came into the warmth of the kitchen from the cold
outside, there wasn't so much as a hint of red in his cheeks. But
he pretended like it was nothing. He expected to work until the
day he keeled over . . .
But it wouldn't help. If I'd ever gotten seriously ill, they would
have cured me of whatever it was before I even knew my disease's
name, no matter how much I protested. No, no, let's not talk
about it. I'll never lie down on one of their operating tables,
not even if there's acute pain in my abdomen. I'll see the face
of God before I see that terrible operating-theater light of theirs
ever again. If I could do it all over again, I'd be a surgeon. Then
I would feel safe. Then it would be me towering above someone
down on my table . . . But it's too late . . . It's too late to make
changes . . . I hate changes, I want everything to stay like it is . . .

Really? Is that what I want? It's awful. Here I sit. The peace I feel, sitting here, is my biggest self-deception. I cling to it. I know that I wouldn't be able to manage if I lost it. Is it still peace if you're terrified to lose it, if you're constantly clinging to it? I don't know what's going to happen from one minute to the next . . . I have nothing to regret. There's nothing I should have said. They can do what they want with me. They can come whenever they want and start to cut me up . . .

I'm becoming scared again now, I think. Now I'm scared. Terribly scared. Aren't there any pills you can take for fear? Something that kicks in almost immediately?

I'm most afraid of becoming afraid again. If I stay scared long enough, it'll turn into panic, and panic is the worst that can happen to someone who's stuck sitting here like this . . .

Yes, I'm becoming scared again . . .

But I can't be afraid . . .

Someone, turn on the light! Turn on the light! I want to see! I want to see you! Stop! Enough! The game's over now! I give up . . . Someone, turn on the goddamn light! Fuck . . . need to keep from panicking . . . I hop from one thought to the other too fast, too quickly for me to keep up, no matter how still I keep my body it's still full speed ahead up here . . . But it all slips away from me, I can't control it, can't watch myself every minute, that's the worst, and some dangerous thoughts slip through, I don't know why it's like that, maybe because it all happens so fast. I don't get it. I can't manage to get a grip before it's too late. It's there, and then it's gone . . .

These thoughts . . .

They shine. And that's what bothers me. Despite everything, they're me at my very best . . .

But only here, in the thoughts that never come to anything. My brightest moments belong to the dark . . .

Shit . . . I make a fool of myself whenever I think. Every single thought I have is an insult to what I might have imagined if only I was up to it. The shit spreads out like the worms wriggling under a stone, under the weight of everything I think about, everything I can't be. I use up all of my strength on this shit, everything that happens in my head is a painful parody of what it might have been. The whole world would have held its breath if only I'd managed to put my thoughts into words, if I could have found the right words to think . . . but my powers slip farther away with each passing day . . .

Sometimes I think that my brain has a brain of its own, it can't just be me who's sending myself all of these messages, who's ordering my thoughts away on these pathetic missions, who's regaling me with these idiotic impressions, stranding me in all this confusion, really, it can't all be coming from me, can it? What do these endless speculations have to do with me? Who is it I think I am?

What influence do I have over what's said? I don't know the difference between a period and a comma, a question mark or exclamation point . . . I can't see whether one or the other is being used . . . Maybe that little extra brain of mine also has a brain of its own? Even smaller but all the more powerful for that, a tiny little devil brain, furrowed and hard like a dried pea . . . and, in reality, it's the one behind everything . . .

and of course, it too has a brain of its own, the smallest and evilest of all . . .

I could have been a great person . . .

If I only . . .

If only I'd been able to concentrate long enough . . .

It would have come, eventually, I'm sure of it . . .

Yes, it would've had to come, in the end, greatness . . .

Fully formed, with everything that goes along with it . . .

But it's too late, I'm too weak, I'm too old, I didn't take the chance when I had it, and now I'm full of shit, my head is full of shit, my thoughts are as black as the shit that came out of old Mrs. Gundersen in room three . . .

There's almost no one like me left, no one who just sits and thinks, who does nothing else but that. I'm the last thinker. A member of a dying species. And my thinking is under attack from all sides. No one wants to let me carry my thought through to completion. They're all afraid that my thoughts will destroy everything they've built their existences on, everything that they believe in and depend on to get them through the day. They all know I'd see right through them if I was allowed to follow my thinking through to its natural conclusions . . . the world is sick . . .

If it hadn't been for Sweetie, I would be much farther along than I am. Maybe I would even have reached my goal by now, would have reached the end of the path, where the final piece falls into place, and everything becomes clear . . . everything which, from that day forward, becomes self-evident, stands as a matter of course . . . A matter of course, that is, for the initiate, for the man who's reached the end of the path, but a mystery for everyone else . . . Yes, I would have managed it by now if it hadn't been for my little darling, busting in here at all hours. A painstakingly constructed argument doesn't mean a thing to her. She doesn't even know what it is. She has no concept of the effort that goes into sustaining it. She thinks you can just pick up the thread wherever you happened to drop it. She thinks thought can be turned on and off like a television . . .

It's impossible to concentrate knowing she's around. I just sit and wait for the door to open, knowing that she'll blow through here like an icy wind, that she'll lift up her nightgown and sit down on the toilet, she has no inhibitions in here, my Sweetie, she just lets it all out, like she was the only person on Earth. Her presence irritates me almost as much as her absence. It makes no difference whether she's here or not. She's always here, regardless. I could be right on the verge of finding the solution to a complicated problem, one it's taken me maybe half a day to so much as determine the basic premises for, and then she'll suddenly barge in to piss or shit, yes, every time, without fail . . .

That fucking bitch! I hear her all the time, she never lets me have any peace. She's my devil, my tormentor. She seduces away my thoughts with all of her noise. There's no one in the whole world who makes as much noise as she does. How the hell does she manage to make so much noise so easily? Maybe she makes so much noise because she can't hear it herself . . . Or maybe she makes noise simply to hear the sound of it. That could be. It must be reassuring to hear the sounds of everything you do. If not, whatever you did might seem completely meaningless. So she clatters, she bangs, she coughs, she clears her throat, she sniffles all the time. I can hear her sniffles day and night, regardless of what room she happens to be in. And the door squeaks horribly whenever she opens it. I've asked her to oil the hinges. She puffs like a whale whenever she washes her face and neck, and when she brushes her teeth, it's like there is something boiling in her mouth. There's even a kind of groan that comes from down between her thighs when she's finished there. Yes, her asshole closes itself with a sigh of self-pity . . .

But if I shout at her, as a rule, it doesn't do a bit of good, even when I know for a fact that she's nearby. I can yell her name as loudly as I like, and then, a moment later, I hear the vacuum cleaner going full blast . . .

Goddamn her! She never comes when I need her, only when I want to be left alone, left in peace. Deafness is a much greater defense against the world than blindness! If you're almost totally blind, there's not much that escapes your notice. But if, on the other hand, you can't hear, you can, if you like, ignore just about anything . . . They wanted to station me on the toilet at first, she and Doctor Amonsen, because then they wouldn't have to give me another thought, I'd be self-sufficient, and it wasn't in my best interest to argue with them, though I preferred the rocking chair. If I wasn't able to rock, what else would I do with myself during the considerable number of years, if it came to the worst, that I might be stuck sitting there? But the discussion worked itself out. If I was on the toilet, where would Sweetie go to the bathroom? It was thanks to that bit of reasoning, I think, that they decided to go with the rocking chair after all. I was surprised at how easily that went . . .

It's important to keep your cells in motion. Two or three meat-balls are all I need to keep my brain functioning. If I eat more than that, I get a headache and fart so much that I think I'll burst . . . I simply can't tolerate pork, it goes right to my heart . . . and Sweetie won't let me take anything for a headache, she thinks that I have enough pills inside of me already . . .

De-Sarg once said . . . he loved to talk in platitudes . . . that you can't just change cars every time your engine stalls. What a terrible analogy. But I've still heard that there are people who went crazy just because their brains got too hot. They simply boiled over, so to speak . . .

Yes, that priceless sponge of mine, weighing just two or three pounds . . . my oldest friend . . . it's gotten me out of a number of difficult situations . . . How wonderful that you can use it to believe that you know so much about yourself, while it, for its part, manages to remain a complete mystery . . .

Sweetie nags at me. You should use your head for something better, she says. She's always sticking her nose into everything I do, no matter how insignificant. She compliments me at the same time, hoping I'll allow myself to be convinced, convinced of whatever it is she wants to convince me. Every time she says that, use your head, I picture a young boy kicking it so hard that it flies in a high arc over a soccer goal. I have to use—how does she put

it?—my resources more effectively. I have to use my thoughts in some other way. She talks like she's been taking classes on the subject. But what other way? Whenever I ask her that, she goes quiet. At least then she doesn't bitch at me for a while . . .
Sweetie doesn't understand this sort of thing. She thinks it's simply a matter of picking out what to concentrate on and what to reject, focusing on constructive things and putting all the rest behind you . . . It's not her fault. She's never experienced anything that might have taught her that it isn't like that. She thinks everything is peaches and cream. She thinks that life is the greatest gift of all. She's like a mouse in a cage. She can't conceive of things being any other way than how she's used to them, there in her nice little cage . . .

De-Sarg was Swiss, he hated weekends, he didn't see the point of them, he let out a sigh of relief every Monday morning when we all got together for our first meeting and the whole week was there stretching out ahead of him, five whole days with every minute already spoken for, filled with so many work responsibilities it felt like it would never end . . . and for him, it never really did. He was probably an example of what men will be like in the next century . . . no time for rest, no desire for rest, always something waiting to be done . . . De-Sarg went, so to speak, from one problem to the next, and I think he was happiest, in fact, when he fell behind, when unfinished tasks began piling up, yes, he loved to feel like there was too much to do, that it couldn't ever be finished, it was a kind of security for him, a kind of insurance, he was only really at ease when he could say to himself that there were still plenty of things he hadn't gotten around to yet . . .
I'd never seen anyone work at such an even and peaceful pace. Not slowly, but not particularly fast either . . . just a frightening ease in all of his movements, like he'd somehow managed to reduce all of his activities to a single steady velocity, the same

speed all the time, no matter what he was doing, as though he was afraid to move too fast, afraid of sabotaging himself by finishing too much at once, that's what he wanted to avoid most of all. I know that the day De-Sarg finds himself standing there with nothing else to work on, finds himself finished with everything he's supposed to do, when there isn't a single task left for him to throw himself into, that's the day De-Sarg will drop dead. He'll fall apart right there and then. He wouldn't be able to stand it. And I guess he must've felt that day coming closer and closer . . . He was a miserable little whiner, making every little thing he did up there at Kronsæther seem like a huge sacrifice on his part, something he'd gone to great lengths to achieve, even though he was paid every fourteenth day just like the rest of us. He approached every tiny job as though it were herculean. He used hair tonic, too . . . the smell remained in the room even after he'd left, an invisible trail telling us where he'd been spending his time. The smell was so strong that I used to wonder, even though I knew it wasn't true, whether he was actually trying to cover up a smell that was even worse . . .

He looked just like one of us, in his white coat. I had plans to get it changed to blue. In blue, his role would be more clearly defined. He caused enough confusion as it was. But I never managed to do anything about it. It was one of those things you think about, from time to time, but never manage to see through . . .

That tight-fisted bastard owed me five hundred crowns by the time I finished working up at Kronsæther. It obviously didn't weigh too heavily on his conscience since he never bothered to contact me about it. He knew I'd never show my face around that fortress of suffering again, so he knew he was safe. If I did show up, unexpectedly, though, I bet he would've forked it all over at once. Maybe he even had the money set aside up there, for all I know. That's how he was. It was how he always managed to

wriggle himself out of trouble. He always had a backup plan . . .
De-Sarg talked all the time, that was the hardest part about being
near him, yes, being in the same room as him . . .
I can hardly bear to think about it . . .
I'll chew a pellet of Orbit gum, that usually helps, absolutely, it
cleans my brain out, it's like an arctic breeze . . . Sweetie takes
care of my supplies, things like gum, consistently, abundantly, I
don't think I've ever reached out toward the dresser and found
my stock empty . . . Oh, maybe it's happened once or twice, but
I can't think of a particular instance . . . Far as I can remember,
things are always the same . . .
Sweetie explained that every flavor has a particular color, like
yellow, green, red, blue. She tried to drill that into me. She got
me to take one, chosen at random. Then she told me what color
it was. Then I took one more, and she told me what color it was.
I never managed to remember which color was which flavor,
though. Finally she gave up. Really, I think that green applies
equally well to any of the available flavors . . .
They squish so effortlessly between my teeth, these small pillows
of gum. And they each contain a refreshing syrup that runs down
into my stomach, small streams that form a river, a river that
sends fresh breath streaming up my throat again . . . it's almost
like fresh flowers are growing down there in my stomach . . .
then I spit the gum out, after a while, once the flavor disappears.
I used to take the wads out with my fingers and stick them to my
rocking chair's armrests or press them under its seat, but they just
stuck to my fingers. I sat there like a rabbit and gnawed for hours
to get them off. Then I tried spitting the globs directly onto my
fingers, but that didn't solve the problem . . . I decided the best
way was just to spit the pieces of gum right out into the air. I tilt
my head back and spit in a high arc to send them as far away as
possible. I hate the thought of them landing in my lap . . . I go
through a couple of packs every two hours. I end up with a blob

the size of a tennis ball. I can barely move my jaw . . .

I reach my hand out for a new pellet. I'm just as excited every single time . . .

A slick new package exactly so many inches long. I've developed my own technique of pressing my thumb into a pack in such a way that the pellets come shooting out of it, one after the other. Whenever I sit like this with a new pack between my fingers, it's like rubbing my hands along a tiny spine . . .

That's what they did when they heard the end was near for their beloved elder relatives, yes, they came to drool over them, licking their lips, running their hands over everything, every Sunday, antiquarians watching their precious investments mature . . . They looked at Kronsæther like it was some kind of safe-deposit box for their treasures . . . Their eyes taking in each detail of their relatives' faces as they sat in the common room every Sunday . . . appraising their value . . .

They were grotesque, especially all made-up like that for visitors' day, big stiff pieces of meat dressed in brocade and chiffon. I don't know if it ever dawned on them, the horrible disparity between owning as much as they did and being in such a fragile state . . . just as old and decrepit as the rest of our patients, money or no money . . . small wet spots blossoming on the backs of their gowns . . . we had to make sure they didn't rot . . .

Why should we have to take care of them, why should they be allowed to move into Kronsæther and eat into our time and re-sources when they were good for hundreds of thousands, or even millions? But their family members were willing to do whatever was necessary to defend their interests . . . they had to keep their investments safe . . . Otherwise these might not pay off when it came time to read the will. It really pissed me off, and it still pisses me off, knowing how many people slip through the cracks and then how many people don't have to. But what could I do? The chairman and the board decided who we took in and who we turned away . . . though really, in practice, it was only the chairman. I had no say in it. Still, his policy wasn't all bad . . . as a rule, it used to be enough to pick up the phone and mention that you were putting some kind of enormous bequest in your will in order to get a bed with us. Whether or not it was true, most of our patients didn't have too bad a life during their last days . . . But the economy put an end to all that. Not because we didn't have money, but because the board refused to use our money where it could actually do some good . . . According to our administrative board, personnel was the problem, personnel always takes the biggest bite out of your budget, sure, we were the ones who were using up all the money. The chairman was always saying that it would be dangerous if we had too much to work with. We'd become far too generous. The perfect situation, if I understood him correctly, was to always have a little less than one needs. As for me, I worked in a drafty office in the western wing, which had never been properly insulated. They tried several times to spray a kind of insulating foam into the walls, but it didn't help. We could only do so much . . . if we tampered with the walls too often, the whole place would've caved in . . . They should have been grateful I stayed. When I look back on it, it occurs to me that I did a fairly good job up there, all things considered . . . My meetings with the board were the real hell. Bourgeois idiots, every last one of them, with a tradition, going back several generations, of sitting around and letting themselves get sidetracked by meaningless details. A curtain committee, that's what it was. What I mean is that if one of our monthly meetings got a little too quiet, if there was an uncomfortable pause, one of them would suggest changing the boardroom curtains, maybe picking out something with a livelier pattern . . . or else they began to discuss the sunny Monets that they'd hung in the hallway. That was the board's gift to us, to frustrate us, to turn down every one of our requests, regardless of how well or badly we did our jobs.

All they knew how to do was criticize, criticize everything, because it was only through this continual criticism that they could justify themselves as being an indispensable part of our operation. They were scared to death. The day they didn't have anything to point their fingers at, someone might have figured out that they served no useful purpose . . .

They loved to use the word liquidity. Yes, that was their enthusiastic refrain at our meetings. The word released a terrible stench into the air, yes, so much so that I was tempted to ask them to remember where we were, to keep themselves from becoming quite so liquid . . .

They prided themselves in having an understanding of absolutely everything. They were on us like vultures whenever I brought up some new, unremarkable statistic. For instance, the death rate grew steadily and consistently during my first years in charge. Eventually it stabilized . . . although, admittedly, at a higher level than before. The board decided that this must have been due to neglect, yes, someone had been negligent . . . an accusation they put forward because they felt they had to, but at the same time, an accusation they knew they didn't have enough evidence to pursue. Time after time, I tried to explain it to them . . . that's what old people do, after all . . . they die. I saw the death rate increase as the most natural thing in the world. Even a lucky break, as far as the staff was concerned . . . something I told my subordinates quite plainly . . .

In any event, thanks to budget cuts, we couldn't bathe everyone regularly. Certainly not all on the same day. We had to make due with the manpower and the resources we had. It was necessary to prioritize. It was awful. It usually didn't take more than a couple of days before our patients were covered in filth. I've never seen anyone get so dirty so quickly as those poor old creatures. Two days without supervision and they looked like mummies, wrapped from head to toe in putrescence. It was almost unbelievable how much waste matter their bodies managed to dispose of in such a short amount of time. Their skin used to flake off like a kind of black confetti. And their smaller, long-standing wounds became almost impossible to find again in all the muck. Even when the nurses knew approximately where on their bodies to look . . .

When I began, the all-quiet signal sounded at eleven o'clock every evening. A few years later, it was changed to ten, and then finally it became nine. And even then we still didn't have enough personnel to get everyone to the toilets and then back to bed again before lights out. We had to prioritize here too. Bladders were emptied wing by wing. The rest had to use what was left of their sphincter muscles to hold it until the sun came up again . . .

My mother was there for seven days before she died. I didn't want her there, not for anything, but the chairman, that son of a bitch, offered to move her there as a special favor when one of our rooms, one of the very best, with a view of the park, became available one night. He was so pleased by his own generosity that I felt it would have been ungracious of me to say no thank you. I saw no way out of the situation. I sent a car for her and got her a bed in room twenty, at the end of the wing where I had my office. It was only a two-minute walk between her and me. Fortunately, things had deteriorated to the point where she rarely recognized me. Most of the time, she had no idea who I was. Not even that I was the managing director . . .

One morning, I went in to her. I couldn't help myself. I wanted to see her before she woke up. I wanted to see her one last time before she went to sleep forever. In my impatience, it hadn't occurred to me that I might as well see her awake, standing at her door, as lying peacefully in her bed. It didn't make any difference. It was as though all my knowledge and experience of these unpleasant creatures was inaccessible when it came to my own mother. Nevertheless, despite my position, I couldn't afford to see her any differently than all the other poor, confused souls at the

institution. She and they were indistinguishable in any case . . .
I put my hand on the doorknob, and the door opened almost by
itself. For a moment, I thought that I had made a mistake. But
then I understood. It was her. She sat on the edge of her bed,
hunched over with nothing covering her top. Her breasts looked
like punctured water blisters. Her arms were in her lap, completely slack. She turned her head toward me, but didn't manage to
cover herself. She just smiled, and that was the worst thing . . .

I DIDN'T HEAR what he said at first. I stood there with his plate in my hand and was going to give it to him. But then he repeated it, that there was something in there, something alive, rustling around, almost imperceptibly, but there nevertheless. Having learned from experience, I let him know that I took this seriously. I put the plate on the dresser and explained to him that the only place something like that could have come from was either the drain or the vent in the ceiling, and that in either case it would have to be very, very small. A spider, maybe. Or an ant. He insisted that I find it for him, that I tell him what it was, and afterward that I make sure to kill it. It was driving him crazy with its barely noticeable rustling. It had been doing it all night, he insisted. I decided not to discuss it with him any further. I kicked a few chewing gum wrappers to one side and tried to make it sound like I was going over every square inch of the floor.

"Are you finding anything?" he shouted. "Are you finding anything?"

I replied that he had to be patient. It could take hours to find a little insect in all of the garbage that was on the floor around him, assuming it was even possible, I said. He had given the little creature a thousand places to hide itself.

But he wouldn't give up: "I know you'll find it. I depend on you, Erna. I depend on you!" His beard hobbled like an animal in his lap whenever he spoke. "You're cleaning up, cleaning it all up, aren't you, my dear?"

I bent down. I panted. I squatted. I was out of breath when I stood up again. I had to sound like I was really putting my heart into it. There were thousands of wads of chewed-up gum under the piles of paper wrappers, big wads and small, stuck to the tiles, especially in the area right around his chair. He just spits them out when he's finished chewing. I'll have to get it really clean in there one day. I'm worried all the gum will clump together. I should begin airing the bathroom out everyday, too. I should leave the window open for at least an hour a day. It'll be completely impossible to breathe in there, soon. The farther you go into the bathroom, the stronger the smell is. I've never worked out what it is, exactly. It's a combination of something very familiar and something entirely alien. Acrid, but with a hint of sweetness, kind of like candy.

"Did you find it?" he asked again. I could tell from his tone of voice that his mood was deteriorating. I told him it wasn't so easy.

"There aren't really so many places it could be, are there?" he asked. He curled up in his chair like someone getting ready to spring into action.

"You can do it, can't you Erna?"

I was up to my ankles in foil wrappers, and they rustled whenever I moved.

"Yes!" he shouted when he heard the noise I was making. "Yes! Exterminate it now! Kill it! Kill it! Listen to me! Kill it!" he shouted and began to rock in his chair, rock for all he was worth. His knuckles whitened as he gripped the armrests.

"Kill it! Kill it! Kill it!" he screamed. The chairs rockers grated against the floor, his head rushing through the air with his hair trailing behind.

"Crush the bastard! Come on, you cunt! Crush it!"

Finally I stamped hard on the floor, thinking it would calm him down, and shouted, "There! There! Yes!" And he did begin to calm down. He was so worn out, he probably wouldn't have been able to go on like that for very long anyway. He sighed like a dog. He stopped rocking and leaned back into his chair, totally exhausted.

"Did you get it?" he whispered.

I acted like I hadn't heard him. "So, you've met your end at last, little bug," I said, sounding just as worn out as Edwin was, and not feeling too much better. I had stepped on one of his old wads of his gum—and discovered this when I lifted my foot. It clung to the sole of my shoe with its thick tentacles. I had to bend over and pry it loose with my fingernails. A little bit stayed stuck under my nail. I rolled it around between my fingers and held it up to the light. Without really thinking about it, I had played my role to perfection, convincing Edwin in the process.

"What was it?" he asked. I told him that it was a tiny spider. I described it in detail. Then I walked over to the sink and washed away my sticky little fantasy.

I put the dinner plate in his lap and told him to hurry up and eat before his food got cold. Then I climbed up and sat down on the toilet. I'd almost forgotten what I really went in there for. The seat is too high for me. I keep a little footstool there. It's my little stairway to heaven.

"Do you wish I was dead?" he asked while he chewed on his first mouthful of food. It seems like he still enjoys eating, despite everything. He smacks his lips loudly. He won't listen when I tell him it's rude. "Yes, it would be best for you if I wasn't here," he said and swallowed. "Then you wouldn't have to worry about me. It would have been better for you, Erna, if you'd had these years to yourself, instead of having to look after a poor old bastard like me, who can't even manage to lift a fork to his mouth without your help." He's quite capable of wallowing like that for hours. I'm never sure whether he actually means it, or if he just wants to be contradicted.

"How's it coming?" he asked. He must have been in a pretty good mood—he set his silverware down, fork and knife together, neatly across his plate, just like he used to do before.

"Is anything coming?"

I didn't answer.

"We should be happy," he said, just as cheerfully. "It would be worse if nothing was coming."

I looked at him. His head stuck up above the back of the rocking chair—round, like a shiny ball—the gray hairs seeming like they were growing into him, not out of him. I got dizzy at the thought of everything that goes on in that head of his—as lifeless as it seems, as still as he sits. It's laughable, the stiffness and motionlessness of his little body, almost invisible under that beard, and then the swarming life up there—in that quivering ball, no bigger than two fists pressed together. I could hardly believe it.

"What day is it today?" he asked.

I had to think about it before I answered.

"Oh. And what day was it yesterday?"

Was this some kind of game? Was he trying to test me?

"Right. Well, there, you see," he said, in his most didactic tone, "everything is fine. Time flies even when we aren't able to follow along so well anymore."

Who was that meant for, him or me? Next he asked what time of year it was. I said that Christmas would be coming soon—I wanted to see if he would argue with me about this—but he seemed to accept it without giving it much thought. It was so easy I almost began to wonder whether I might have been telling the truth.

"How old am I now? Do you remember?

"Old," I replied.

"And how long have I been sitting here?"

"A long time," I answered.

I didn't have the energy for it. When he's feeling talkative, he doesn't seem to care whether or not I hold up my end of a conversation. I used to lie to him on his birthdays when he would ask if any cards had arrived. I read telegrams to him that I had written myself, repeated phone conversations that I dreamed up on the spot. Finally, I avoided mentioning his birthday entirely. It didn't really make any difference whether a month or a year had gone by. He didn't notice anyway.

"Do you ever miss the time when everything happened by itself, when we didn't need to think about anything?" he asked.

I didn't know what to say. He must have heard me. I couldn't help it. I was always letting out these small groans. Maybe he was just hoping to drown out my own thoughts with his questions?

"Is there a draft on you?" I asked. I noticed that his shirt was riding up, which it always does after he's been awake a few hours. He didn't answer. The bathroom door doesn't reach all the way down—probably designed that way to reduce humidity in the room, but it lets in a lot of cold air. All it takes is for the kitchen window to be open a couple of minutes. Cold drafts in a humid room cause so many of the world's illnesses. Especially for someone who sits as still and is as inactive as Edwin. I'll call the super and ask him to come and have a look. Maybe he might be able to do something about it? Edwin's shirt rides up in the back, mostly—I mean his sweat suit, which is just too small for him now. It's always creeping upwards—even the tiniest movement makes a big gap at the small of his back where the cold air can get in. I tuck his shirt in, pull his jacket down over it, and straighten him up as best I can between the spindles that make up the back of the rocking chair. Of course, the next time I go in there, it'll all be just as bad. Everything is always in complete disarray. It's a good thing he has his slippers. They keep his ankles warm. Once your ankles get cold, you might as well give up trying to keep the rest of your body warm.

"The days are long, aren't they?" he asked. "Don't you wish you had someone here who could keep you company? Couldn't Sigri come and help you out a little? I mean in here, with me. Once or twice a week? Of course, it's not the best way to do things, but otherwise it's just the two of us all the time. Hasn't it been a little while since Sigri was last here? I don't think I've heard her for a while now. Is she sick?"

I explained that Sigri usually comes once a week. It had been almost a week since she was last here.

"Which day does she usually come?"

I told him, even though I was sure that he already knew.

"Has it always been the same day? Wasn't it a different day to begin with?"

I couldn't answer with certainty that it hadn't been.

"I think that it was," he said quickly. "I wonder if it wasn't on Fridays that she used to come, originally. You should ask her about that, the next time she comes. Things like that are useful to know. How long has it been since we first hired her?"

I said that it was a bit strange to put it like that, that we'd hired Sigri, since she could hardly be called an employee, she only comes around once a week to help with the shopping.

"Are you keeping track of her budget? Do you write down how much she spends every week? Do you keep the receipts? Have you actually seen them? Maybe she buys things for herself at the same time—have you thought of that? Not that money is everything, but still, it's important, don't you think? Something like that could add up to a fortune over a long period of time. But it's typical of you not to worry yourself about it. So how long has Sigri been working for us, now?"

I responded with a question of my own, hoping to head him

off, asking what exactly he meant, how long.

"Are you sure she always gives you the right change?" he asked, as if he hadn't heard anything I'd just said, even though he brags about having hearing like a dog's. "It's not about the money. It's a matter of principle. How old is she?"

I didn't answer.

"How old is Sigri?"

I said that I didn't know.

"But you must have some idea of her approximate age?"

I answered that it was a little hard to tell with her.

"Take a guess then. Somewhere between what and what?"

I told him that I wouldn't take a guess when I really had no idea. That bothered him, and his chair began to rock a bit again.

"For Gods sake, is she ten or is she forty? Isn't it still possible to look at people and guess their approximate age?"

Well, then I guessed that somewhere between twenty and thirty.

"Money's never been a problem for us, has it?" he asked. "We've never really had debts, we've only ever loaned money to other people, and then only small amounts."

No, that was true, I said.

"We were both moderate and cautious. We managed to get everything to work pretty well. We've been clever. Not everyone can do that."

Since he was talking about our finances, and since he had brought it up, I wanted to mention the chewing gum problem to him, wanted to ask him what he thought it cost us over the course of a year, his sweet tooth. But I knew that he wouldn't pay any attention to me. Presumably, he wouldn't even understand what I was getting at. He asked: "Isn't that true? You've never gone wanting, never felt like there was something you needed that you absolutely couldn't have?"

Oh no, I answered. We've managed quite well.

"We were fortunate," he continued, "that we could inherit our apartment, that we didn't need to borrow any money, that both of us were able to live on a single wage."

I finished up and hopped down. I don't use the footstool when I want to get down, preferring to jump the short distance. When I closed the door behind me, I emerged into the dusk, or it seemed that way after the sterile, hospital-like white of the bathroom: a warm evening with humming insects and lilac bushes giving out their heavy fragrance. I glanced back at the small crack where the door didn't meet the threshold. The bathroom light boiled away through the opening, bubbling and sizzling like acid. I have to call the super about that light. It's unpleasant to be in there while it's on, you see everything too clearly—but I can't get myself to call, even though he was so helpful last time. I'm afraid he'll take it the wrong way if I call and complain about his work. It's been so long since he was here, he would think we'd been suffering in silence this whole time. He might misinterpret my request as serious disapproval. I worry that there's no right way to present the situation to him.

I went around the living room and turned all the lights off, finishing up at the sofa, where I sat down. There's something about the dark that demands quiet. I've noticed that I think differently when I'm out in the apartment, as opposed to when I'm in the bathroom. I often become unsure as soon as I've closed the door behind me whether or not I've actually spoken to Edwin, or whether I've just imagined what he probably would have said, and what I probably would have said in reply. It even happens that I wonder sometimes whether he's actually sitting in there at all . . . whether there's anyone in there . . . whether I'm only imagining things. And besides—the man I think is sitting in there, what does he have to do with the Edwin I used to know? There's something shocking about the fact that he's such a mystery to me . . . my own husband. I've tried to remember how he was, how he looked, but I can't manage it—the old man in the bathroom appears each time I try to picture him. But nonetheless, I can't help but think that the man in that rocking chair, sitting in the bathroom, is Edwin, the same Edwin as before, the same Edwin as always, disguised as a wrinkled old man, peeking out at me through that old man's lifeless eyes. I keep hoping I'll find him sitting there one day without his disguise. I keep hoping I'll find him sitting there one day, waiting for me, smiling—that he'll stand up when I come in and reach out his arms to me. I've forgotten what he looked like, but I know I'll recognize him the moment I see him.

GODDAMN HER! SHE didn't turn the faucet all the way off, she's always doing that, she doesn't care, and it can drip like that for hours! Those little drips turn into explosions after a while . . . the Chinese, I think, used to torture people like that . . . I've shouted to her several times, but there isn't a sound out there, not from any of the rooms . . .

Maybe she's still in here, maybe she's in here with me, been here the whole time, wouldn't surprise me in the least, maybe she's hidden herself somewhere in here, maybe she's sitting and following along with everything I do, for all I know she could even be underneath my chair, and maybe the next time I do a little rocking, the next time I launch myself into a good rocking, I might rock right over an obstruction, an obstruction that could only be her. I'd stop and begin to feel around, and my hand would get tangled in her shawl, that goddamn white knitted shawl that she's worn around her shoulders since we were married, and I'd know that she was lying there, plastered over with a thin layer of sugar-free chewing gum. God knows how long she'll lie there before I notice. It's not at all unlikely . . . she's been complaining about aches and pains here and there, lots of headaches, wheezing, a tightness in her chest . . .

I thought it was strange that I hadn't heard from her the last few days, which I mentioned right away, unless it's only been the last few hours? Naturally, it's her choice whether or not to come in here and clean up a little. I shake her until she pays attention. She huffs and puffs as she gets back on her feet. I've never heard such a racket. It's like she's coming up from swimming laps in the sea of paper on the floor. Obviously she's trying to make what she's been through seem as strenuous as possible . . .

What's the matter with you? I ask. Asking is the least I can do. She answers that she's fine, there isn't a thing wrong, but her tone is unmistakable . . .

Of course, what she's getting at is that she wants me to feel sorry for her, but that's not possible, how can I spare her any sympathy when she's always interrupting me? But still, I'm not stingy. If she doesn't feel well occasionally, that's fine. She's entitled. I owe her that much . . .

She's so small, Sweetie, she almost looks like a dwarf. That's how I remember her, tiny . . . it's been many years since I last was able to see her, but she moved like a penguin even then . . .

One month after our wedding, her shoulders went stiff and started hurting. The doctor told us it was a chronic condition. I felt like I'd been cheated . . .

We should have brought some children into the world, I would have had more to look back on now, both of us would, but nothing ever came of it, neither of us wanted children while it was still possible to have any. I remember she did ask me once if maybe it wouldn't be nice to have some kids running around here at home, I said yes, of course, sure, it would, but in the back of my mind I was praying that she wasn't serious . . .

A liar, that's what you turn into when you're with a woman. You have to lie the whole time. Otherwise, you'd never be able to keep her. Sometimes I was barely able to swallow whatever it was she'd cooked for dinner, but when the meal was over, I always told her

that it tasted great, yes, whatever it was was always delicious . . .
It never made any difference how often she'd swear never to leave
me. I've never really felt secure with her. Whenever I let some
little insinuation slip out, she always interprets it in a completely
baffling way. It's too risky. You have to try as hard as you can to
control yourself. You don't ever want to scream out whatever's
bothering you right in your wife's face . . .

It used to be that I could predict her comings and goings, as a
rule, but not anymore . . . either I've lost the knack, or she's found
a way to fool me . . . the door bursts open all of a sudden and she
comes up to me and tears off my bag without a word, the same
way she'd tear a ticket off the dispenser in line at the bakery . . .
Then, I feel her fingers, quick and sure of themselves, with their
icy tips, almost like lead. It's a good feeling. Then I can just let
go again, she isn't embarrassed, she got over all that a long time
ago . . .
I'll be goddamned if I ever have to live through this life again! I
shout after her when she leaves . . .
But I don't know if she understands what I mean when I talk like
that. I try to keep my spirits up, but of course the first thing she
does when I say things she can't understand is laugh . . . though
this may be because her hearing has deteriorated to the point where
she can't make out the subtle nuances of what I'm saying. I've
always had to put things very simply for her . . . I could never take
anything for granted, always had to explain everything from the
ground up, step by step, otherwise she wouldn't understand what
I'm talking about, so it's clear that I've never made the least bit of
progress with her, that I've never really been able to tell her what
was really in my heart, no, my heart is terra incognita, I've used
up all my time with her starting over from the beginning, over
and over again, the beginning is all she could ever understand,
she thinks there isn't anything more to it than the beginning, she

thinks that I've said everything there is to say to her, when the fact is that I've barely even begun . . .

In the meantime, I'm not entirely convinced, on the subject of her hearing, that it's as weak as she claims it is, since there have been several occasions when I know she's heard something she shouldn't have been able to, like someone clearing his throat, or a casual remark, so, all in all, it seems she just hears what she wants to hear . . . but perhaps that's the case with most people who claim to be hard of hearing. She hears quite well, presumably, but figured out that this so-called handicap of hers is an advantage. Now she's free to pick and choose, she can hear whatever suits her and ignore the rest . . . it comes down to her whims, and naturally no one would ever dare to challenge her on this point, to suggest she might be faking . . .

It was the same story with Mrs. Engstrand, she fluttered around like a lunatic bird in her own little world and wouldn't listen to a single thing we said, though I suspected she was exaggerating her condition . . . finally I took matters into my own hands and gave her the treatment, with an ear syringe I mean, and then it just ran out of her, huge pieces of earwax looking like homemade caramel. She shook her head. The first thing I said to her afterward, in a normal tone of voice, was How did it feel? And then she blushed, the old crank . . . who'd have thought there was any blood left in those gray pancakes she called cheeks?

If I'd had the strength for it, I'd give Sweetie the same treatment . . . But I've studied the subject, conducted a few small experiments. I shout to her, first quietly, then, gradually, louder, until I'm screaming like a hysterical woman. Some days I don't have to keep it up as long as others . . . and that's what's so interesting. Sometimes she hears me on the fourth or fifth shout . . . others, I get seven or eight. It's even happened that I've reached ten shouts before I finally hear chair legs scraping against the floor out there and then that little squeak when my door swings open, and I know she's in front of me with her stooped shoulders, one hand on the doorknob . . .

Does light come into the bathroom when she opens the door? No, of course it doesn't. Quite the opposite. I never hear her turn the apartment lights on or off. And if she ever turned the bathroom lights off, I'd notice it right away, since the constant buzzing from that horny bastard's fluorescent tube would stop. It's even louder now than it was before he came. And she leaves the water running all the time. How nice of her, when she knows I live through my ears. I hope she's taken the trouble to find out whether it's dangerous to leave the water running. I have no idea what it does to the pipes. Maybe they explode if you never turn off the flow . . .

If the eyes are the windows of the soul, what does that say about me, Edwin Mortens, and my small, gray, cloudy eyes? Someone could drive nails through them without my even noticing. As a rule, the kids responsible for our residents with vision problems always took enormous liberties . . . they were negligent, washed their charges less carefully, and showed less consideration to them than they did to the ones who could see. They didn't care, didn't have to care, had bad attitudes, didn't like to answer my questions . . . God help me. A man who's all alone and can't stand on his own two legs. Sweetie told me once that British scientists managed to clone a sheep. They made a whole new sheep from only a single cell, so the new sheep is just like the original sheep right down to the last tuft of wool. So, suddenly, we have two of the same sheep. I have no idea how they did it. She didn't say anything about that. According to Sweetie, they can do the same thing with people now, if they want. The principle is basically the same . . . Oh, that would be priceless, wouldn't it, my dear . . . Are you here now, listening? Just think, the day of my funeral, you come home, breathing a sigh of relief, you pull off your veil, you go into the bathroom to wash off your make-up, only to find another Edwin sitting here . . .

In the old days there was always a little puff of hot air when a bit of shit came out of me, but now it just feels cold, it just pours out of my freezing asshole and right into the bag, I miss the feeling of passing something solid down there. I've said to Sweetie that it's an awful lot of work for us both when you remember it's something that should really happen by itself. I guess as long as I'm not shitting money we'll just have to go on doing whatever we need to in order to get rid of the stuff . . .

I used to feel healthy, agile, didn't have any problems for years, but then I started to feel like I had to take a piss pretty much all the time, like my body was full of urine, like I even had to piss out of my fingertips. Amonsen advised me to take it easy and stay as still as possible, or else, conversely, suggested that I ought to get more exercise . . . I don't remember anymore. But there were pills for it too, and then, later, the catheter, and then the problem went away, everything was working again, just like it should, almost as well as nature originally intended . . .

The catheter made me think of old Miss Prytz, who tried to teach us brats some German . . . utterly hopeless, despite the old bitch's tenacity. *Guten Tag, meine Frau. Vielen Dank. Bitte schön* . . .

Everyone could abandon me, but I'd still be here when they got back, no matter how long they were away, and even though they would assume I must have died while they were gone, as soon as they try to stow my carcass in the dirt, I'll open my eyes and stick out my tongue, stretch it out at them, and the communion wafers will all stick in their throats, those hypocritical dregs of society. They all want to segregate the dead from the living, but things aren't that simple anymore . . .

I wonder what Sweetie thinks of me, the fact that I never do anything but sit here. She must have given up all hope for me a long time ago . . . or no, it's only that the nature of her hope has evolved with time . . . before she always hoped that there might still be a little life left in me, but now she just hopes that whatever spark of life I've got will be extinguished as soon as possible, so she can be done with me at last, and maybe have a few good years left for herself, which is, after all, no more than she deserves, no, it's no more than she deserves . . .

I have two fingernails I need to ask her to do something about, they've started to become ingrown on both my thumbs, they are slicing into the skin there like two little knives . . .

There is nothing much in me. I only drink what I need to keep from drying out completely. Cola, for the most part. The water here isn't really fit to drink . . . it turns to sludge in my throat. Whenever she comes in here with a mug of cola I hear it sputtering, crackling, and popping, just like real fireworks . . . it's like I feel a cold but comfortable gust of fresh air when she sets the mug down on the dresser, it cools me off. I usually wait until the fireworks have calmed down a bit in order to drink my cola, most of the carbonation needs to be gone before I feel I can really enjoy my drink, the carbonation shouldn't snap, it should doze, and I prefer my soda lukewarm . . . then, it becomes like the remnant of something rare, something holy . . .

I don't eat especially much either, about the only thing I take now and then is a meatball, just to calm my stomach down. Really, I'd rather just get fed intravenously, since then I wouldn't have to lift a finger . . . it could flow into me the same way it flows out. There's plenty of room, we could clear a nice space for it here, next to me, the stand for the I.V. bag and everything. I've talked with Dr. Amonsen about it, but even though he assured me that he was on my side, he let it be known that it wasn't really an option, that no one would take such a request seriously from someone who could still eat normally, that the people who sit and make decisions as to who gets what equipment would never approve. I'd best forget about it, he told me, unless I wanted to cast myself in an unpleasant light. I told him that I had a bit of experience with people like that myself, to show that I understood . . .

That's what you get for following the rules all your life. Really, the law is the last thing you ought to worry about. It's not there to help us, after all, but to control us . . .

I have no idea what it is, but I know there must be something, some kind of machine, that could make my life easier, that could simplify my responsibilities, and make things easier for Sweetie too, she's the one who needs the most help, really. There isn't anything that they don't make, they even have a device to open a person's mouth and then another to close it again. Mr. Gud-medstad had a magnifying glass mounted on his chair so he could see what he was eating and maneuver it into his mouth, but as soon as it was installed, women always avoided him, they were scared to death of what he might be scrutinizing through his little glass, even though they all knew what it was there for . . .

I can do whatever I want, of course. In here, all my thoughts come true, something that's never happened to me before, I've never seen anything I wanted actually come to pass, but now all I have to do is think and things are just as I want them. This rocking chair is my throne . . . I run everything from here. I am absolute ruler over my own kingdom . . . in the monarchy of my thoughts . . .

I see I'm in a good mood today. I want to do everything I can to keep myself this way. A tab of Orbit gum helps me to hang on to that feeling . . . I don't give a damn what color it is . . . There we go . . . chewing, chewing . . .

I'm wonderful, I have to admit it, I've got nothing to complain about. I have a bottle that I piss in and a bag that I shit in. I don't need to exert myself over anything. This body is so stiff from arthritis that it even sits by itself. I feel that I've accomplished everything I needed to in life, if not more. This is the supreme

moment . . . I wouldn't be opposed to dropping dead right here and now. And there's so much more to be thankful for . . . I can listen to whatever I want . . . I can yell at people, can say anything that comes into my head . . . I can give a real earful to whoever I want . . . can bitch at the prime minister, insult the king, and tell dirty jokes to the queen . . . yes, I can get away with everything I've ever wanted, and without having to be the least bit responsible for my actions . . . I could even become a surgeon if I wanted . . . why not? . . . in nice green surgical scrubs . . . I could go out and slice people up to my heart's content, do whatever I want to whoever I want, open them up from top to bottom, put my hands in their guts, cut some bits out, tear a few things in two, and even sew them back together again, if the spirit moves me . . .
One more pellet, they've never tasted better . . .
And it wouldn't make any difference if I made any mistakes, it's impossible to take doctors to court for anything, they're like the police, they all just look out for their own kind, and they're good at covering up for one another . . . they operate on a level where the layman isn't just considered a layman, but an ignorant, idiotic, worthless chump . . .
What a joy it would've been for that old bookkeeper father of mine. His son, a surgeon. From what I understand, he'd always hoped I'd be a doctor. Of course, he thought that he'd made that clear to me . . . but he was too much of a mystery in life for me to figure out what he actually expected of his son . . .
One more pellet . . .
When I was fourteen, I played the trumpet . . . I don't remember whether it was with or without my father's blessing. Some guy whose name I've forgotten and who called himself a music teacher or anyway had those words engraved on a plaque he'd hung up over the doorbell used to put a metal tube into my mouth and would stand there pouring water down it while he screamed into my ear that I had to learn to blow a little harder. I remember

him as being a less than ideal instructor . . . If I'd had better luck,
I would have managed to strike a better balance between what
came in and what went out . . . but I never became a trumpet
player. The only thing our music teacher really knew about was
reprisals . . . there wasn't anything that would convince him not
to cane us. He even beat us while we played, and we sobbed into
our trumpets, and then he beat us even more because we weren't
playing clearly. His goal was perfection, we had to become the
best trumpet players this world had ever heard . . . either that,
or nothing at all. He used to encourage us by saying, You're all
a bunch of talentless, snot-nosed brats! Look at you monkeys!
You'll never learn to do it right! . . . He laughed at us whenever
we actually tried to improve, and finally his face turned red as
a lobster, and he grabbed all our instruments away and started
playing them himself, imitating us, hitting all the wrong notes.
Presumably, he got what he wanted . . . none of us became
musicians . . .
One more pellet . . . this is a special day . . . I can feel it . . .
Surgeons are at the center of life . . . our lives stop or continue
depending on him . . . we're all equal before the surgeon . . .
generals and financiers have no power over him . . . there's only
one way to meet the surgeon, and that's with complete and entire
submission. Men and women will look me in the eye, awestruck,
terrified . . . their fear will have no bottom . . . and they'll know
that I see right through them . . .
We never understand the power other people have over us until
we're helpless, and then we don't have any say in the matter . . .
you can't choose whom you want to be dependent on. Power isn't
distributed according to knowledge or experience, the only way to
get it is by maneuvering around people, since everyone's got their
own agenda . . . the world's run according to hidden motives . . .
There are a number of things I should have asked the doctor about
through the years, but I never did, despite being on the point

of asking, because I didn't want to give too much away, didn't want to give him complete and unrestricted influence over what I do. If I hadn't managed to control myself, he would have been able to get what every doctor truly wants . . . that is, complete control over their patients' lives. I wouldn't even be able to open my eyes in the morning without Dr. Amonsen having something to say about it . . . And even if he's far from being the worst of them . . . Dr. Amonsen, I mean . . . he's actually one of the very best, in fact . . . there isn't a single place on my body he doesn't have intimate knowledge of. . . he's a master, for instance, when it comes to finding out if a shoe is pinching my foot. Stop eating anything with onions in it, my good man! he told me after making a preliminary examination, so of course I immediately had to take what he said into consideration . . . it was like he'd read my mind, his diagnosis was so insightful, I couldn't help but think I'd have put it in exactly the same way, if I was in his place . . .

Sweetie liked him immediately, she'd put her make-up on if there was the slightest chance he'd be coming by . . .

He was always generous with prescriptions, you only had to complain once and he gave you something right away. Of course I let him understand right from the start that I was terribly impressed with his expertise. Eventually there wasn't anything he wouldn't write me a prescription for . . .

Yes, and I really was impressed. Apparently every affliction known to man comes complete with a countermeasure in the form of a little white pill! They brought me pills in glasses, in cartons, in those little blister packets . . . I always liked the packets best, the rustling of the capsules inside, pressed up against their aluminum foil . . . pushing them out was like popping an abscess, forcing a node out into the air . . .

I became an expert at swallowing pills . . . I didn't even need water. I was able to swallow four or five, one after the other, just using my saliva. I put them all the way back on my tongue, shoved them right down my throat, so to speak . . .

Things were a little more orderly when we first started out, I had a small plastic carousel with little spaces for the pills, and you just had to reach out and touch it to spin it around and make its cargo tumble out, green, yellow, pink, and white, one after the other. I called it my wheel of fortune, and the squeaking it made as it spun was like the sound of coins jingling in my pocket, but I had to stop when my eyesight began to disappear entirely, there was no point in my sitting there and spinning the wheel blindly, who knows what drug I'd end up with, it would have been like playing Russian roulette, that's what Dr. Amonsen said . . . or, anyway, that's what Sweetie told me Dr. Amonsen had said. I have to take her word for it. It bothers me that I can't talk to him directly anymore, that Sweetie gets to decide what to tell me, how much information gets through . . . for all I know only half of the advice he gives has actually reached me, and maybe he's even arranged some tests for me at the hospital that Sweetie hasn't bothered to mention . . . maybe he's even asked permission to admit me . . . maybe there's even a bed waiting for me at this very moment, for God's sake . . .

Either you're dependent on medication, under the supervision of doctors, or you're dependent on a woman, I don't know which is worse . . . from Amonsen at least I always felt there was a certain understanding of the gravity of my situation, but from Sweetie, everything is quotidian, commonplace, she sees me every day, does the same things every day, changes my bag just like she changes the bag in the vacuum cleaner or puts a new filter in the coffeemaker . . . And for every little thing that she helps me with, for every little thing I wouldn't have been able to manage on my own, she spins another invisible thread around me. She's a real nurse with wound, as we used to say up at Kronsæther . . . more interested in helping herself than her patient. I know she's

hidden prescriptions from me, prescriptions Dr. Amonsen wrote
for me and gave to her, prescriptions we'd agreed about, the
doctor and me, for drugs I would have benefited from, but no,
that goddamned bitch, for some bizarre reason or other, decided
that they wouldn't do me any good. I've asked her to hand them
over, but she won't do it. I've demanded that she should give all
my prescriptions to Sigri the next time she comes over, so she
can go to the drugstore and have them filled, but Sweetie still
denies they exist . . .
When I think about what she's probably basing her behavior
toward me on, it almost makes me cry . . . she's the last person
in the world who should assume a position of authority about
anything, after all . . . the only one who knows for certain what's
good for me and what's not good for me is me, it's always been
that way, and it'll be that way until the day Sweetie plants an ax in
my skull, according to my direct orders, my explicit instructions,
that is, on the day I decide that I want an ax in my forehead,
that is, I mean, on the day I say it will happen. Of course, this
all depends on whether she'll be strong enough to lift the thing.
A good ax needs to have a real heft to it in order to get the job
done. I can't stand the thought of any half-hearted attempts.
What I want is a single heavy blow that will split my skull and
brain in two . . .
Goddamn her! She's always laughed at my suffering, waving it
away like it was nothing more than a few harmless gnats . . .
sometimes I think she believes I deserve everything I get . . .
When I first started losing my sight, she put her foot down, was
adamant, wasn't willing to give an inch, heartless as it was, and
I told her so, right to her face, but she didn't believe me, plain
and simple, she thought I was making it up. To underscore her
skepticism as far as my new handicap, she even made sure to
laugh loudly every time I stumbled down a step, when I simply
stepped into air. You sure are a strange one! she used to say, with

a mix of scorn and loving consideration in her voice, though, honestly, the changes I was going through must have been glaringly obvious to her, it all happened so quickly, all at once, like I'd been strapped into a centrifuge and all my good qualities spun right out of me, flying every which way, forced out of me, fluttering off like bits of torn-up paper, and I emerged again, headless, a miserable parody of myself, a naive version, a hopeless case, just like one of my old patients at the home . . . No, Sweetie only started to take it seriously when I showed her the forms from the social security office, when I tossed them on the table in front of her and she read that I could take as many taxis as I wanted and only pay a symbolic amount for each ride, sure, then she finally believed me . . .

I became a shadow of my former self. I became invisible. All I could see after a while was my own gradually diminishing eyesight, my own shrinking world. To lose your eyesight is to lose the faculty with which you make yourself useful. If you can't see what you're doing, you can't manage to accomplish anything. To put it bluntly, you become a bum . . . Edwin, of all people, who was precision itself, who was known for it, notorious for it, who was absolutely meticulous in everything he did. I swear, I never left a single mistake behind in the places I've worked.

I never left anything to chance, I didn't know how else to do things. I always made sure to know everything my employees were working on, and I participated as much as I could in the process to ensure that everything functioned smoothly. My methods were criticized, especially by the department nurses, who thought I was a real pain in the neck, since I was always interfering . . . they complained, and had every right to complain, that an administrator is meant to be an organizer, not a specialist. Nevertheless, I took a special pleasure in knowing everything, or almost everything, in any case . . . as long as I was able to keep track of everything that went on, I felt like the entire operation was something that began with me. I let nothing go unexamined, and under my leadership, our morning reports became intricately filigreed works of art. I became infamous for being unable to delegate, either because I didn't know how, or because I just didn't want to, they were never able to figure it out, but whatever the case, I always had to get a word in about every single decision, right down to the tiniest details. I developed a series of new regulations which then all had to be implemented by me personally before they could be put into general practice, despite the fact that they were all elementally simple. One of the largest parts of this restructuring, which I could easily have let the appropriate department heads worry about, was ensuring that every responsibility had been assigned to the most capable personnel . . . determining medicine dosages, for example, or the ordering of food for the various wings . . . things that now took a great deal longer than if the ward nurses had been allowed to go on doing it all themselves, which they naturally were more than qualified to do. Micromanagement is what De-Sarg called it, acting, as usual, as though he actually knew what he was talking about . . .

One day, however, I had to acknowledge that what I was doing simply didn't interest me anymore. My ability to engage myself with what was happening up at the home had simply disappeared. It was like someone had come in and turned out the light. I found I was no longer able to tell our residents apart . . . their faces no longer set off any memories in me, I didn't have the least sensation of recognition when I looked at them, and it was the same with the older ones, who'd been there a while, as with the younger ones, the recent arrivals . . . and, actually, I couldn't even tell the older ones from the younger ones now. They were simply a mass of anonymous, incurable afflictions. Pronouncing their names correctly became a chore. Everything was an enormous, confusing mess. Then, from one day to the next, I forgot the names of their family members, forgot the details of their therapeutic histories, the results of their most recent tests, forgot all the information it was absolutely necessary to keep in mind in case of emergency. But maybe all this was overdue. I'd already been having trouble, for a while now, deciphering the numbers I wrote down whenever I calculated my statistics. It took me five whole days to prepare a simple account of quarterly management activities, though I pretended I'd just whipped it up in the few minutes it took the board to convene. My mouth became dry, and my eyelids hurt . . . If the occasion had presented itself, I probably would have ended up doing something terrible . . . if, that is, something terrible hadn't managed to find me first . . .

Goddamn it! I had agreed to take a couple of board members around on a guided tour, which was the sort of thing they'd demand once in a while, without warning, so that they could update themselves about our operations, as they put it, making it all sound like an absolute necessity. We had just about finished wending our way through half of our palace of sorrows when one of the nurses showed up with some papers that she needed my signature on . . . she was relatively new, so I tried to be as polite as possible when I explained to her that this wasn't the best time, and that the signature would have to wait. Even an infant would have picked up on the gravity of my demurral . . . but this girl wouldn't give up. The new ones were always so eager. She began to argue with me, saying that it really wouldn't take any time at all, and that it would be better to take care of the papers right away . . .

What irritated me most was that the board members I was showing around took the nurse's side . . . they stepped away and waved their arms at me, signaling that they had nothing against waiting a minute or two if there was something important that needed attending to . . . I tried to control myself, but I was so incredibly angry when the nurse slipped a pen between my fingers, when I took the clipboard and its precious papers from her, that all I could see was a horrible pink cloud floating in front of me, a poisonous cloud, I remember thinking . . .

I asked her where I should sign. She pointed. I held the pen out in front of me. My hand was nothing more than a shadow. I had no choice. I had to make an attempt. But there was something about the whole situation that had thrown off my equilibrium. I wasn't parsing the situation properly. I felt that everything was hopeless, that I'd been condemned . . .

I signed, even though I knew that I was doomed. I started writing and the clipboard disappeared entirely, I'd written right off the edge, the pen making a useless curtsy in the air. I saw that that pushy cunt was staring at me now, terrified. I was shouting at her, she shouldn't have bothered me with these stupid details . . . I announced that I was going to knock her down . . . I hit her so hard that she flew across the slippery floor until she disappeared from view . . .

It was a situation that certainly could have been handled with a little more aplomb, a little more self-possession, not to mention politeness, but now, much to my annoyance, it was blown up into a complete fiasco. Our board members were never exactly discrete . . . they spread the news wherever they went, yelling about every detail . . . unless all their yelling was actually for my benefit . . . maybe once they noticed that my vision was on the way out, they assumed I was going deaf into the bargain. Yes, they made it all sound much worse than it was . . . my head research assistant had even found it necessary to throw himself between the nurse and me, to protect her . . . they were prepared, he said later, on behalf of the community, and in such a way that there could be no misunderstanding as to his intentions, yes, they were prepared to do whatever was necessary to respond to further aggression on my part . . .

"WHERE'S DINNER, WOMAN?" he asked when I went in, the poor man. It was eight o'clock in the morning. The light was flooding over his shoulders like boiling milk. The narrow bathroom window hovered over his head. It was like a chapel in there, with Edwin a holy man, sitting completely still with that long beard of his and those huge slippers, wearing that shiny jogging outfit, someone you'd lay down flowers for, or else make a sacrifice to. His hair shone like gold. I became solemn. It was like he'd been sitting there for a thousand years.

"How old am I now?" he asked. I didn't understand what he was saying at first. He had to repeat it two or three times. It takes longer and longer for his voice to become clear. It's like something is growing down inside of him, blocking his throat, between the times he speaks.

"Old," I said.

"And how long have I been sitting here?"

"A long time," I answered. It was the answer he was used to hearing. What's odd is that he usually accepts it without complaint.

"What day is it today?" he asked. I told him.

"Is Sigri coming today?" he asked next. I answered no, she wasn't, that she was coming tomorrow, and that then, when she came, it would have been a week since she was last here.

"Is she good-looking?" I was somewhat nonplussed by this question. I wasn't sure how to answer.

"Has she changed very much since she began working for us? Has she aged, I mean? How long has she been working for us?"

I told him that he had to stop talking about Sigri as though she were just a maid. Then I remembered that they'd never actually seen one another.

"De-Sarg still owes me five hundred crowns. Did you know that?"

De-Sarg—the name gave me a shock. Edwin used to talk about him all the time, in the old days. He was the one who was responsible for technical services up at the home. I think Edwin admired him, though he wasn't especially fond of him.

"Yeah, that bastard owes me five hundred crowns."

I told him that maybe it would be best if he simply forgot about the money, since he'd never see any of it.

"That son of a bitch owes me five hundred crowns, and he will until the day I die . . . and then all the way up till the day he dies himself. But maybe he's already dead. A sobering thought. Maybe they're putting him into the ground at this very moment."

I didn't know what I should say.

"But the debt remains. It doesn't matter what happens . . . De-Sarg will still owe me five hundred crowns. See what I mean? That's what we'll leave behind, the day we're both lying underground . . . a debt of five hundred crowns. It'll be that way for all eternity, understand? Until it's taken care of, the debt will always remain . . ."

I didn't answer. I didn't think it was anything I should get mixed up in.

"I have a piece of paper with his signature on it in one of the drawers in the kitchen. And it says that he owes me five hundred crowns. Would you see if you can find it for me? I'd really like people to know about it, when I'm gone, that that bastard never settled things between us, that he's lying in his coffin with a black mark on his conscience. I want you to find that paper and make sure to leave it somewhere where it'll definitely be found."

I said that I'd try, but that I couldn't guarantee I'd find the note, considering how disorganized everything was out there. And anyway, what would it matter if neither he nor De-Sarg were alive anymore?

"It's not about the money," he answered. "I just want people to know about it, I want them to see the debt with their own eyes, so go and find it for me, go find that piece of paper right away and bring it here, I want to hold it here in my hand, I want to know that it still exists."

I promised Edwin that I would take care of it, but that it would have to wait a bit. There were other things that I needed to do first. But of course he didn't want to hear about that. In his mind, he's the one who gives the orders, and I'm the one who follows them, not the other way around. But I can't help that things don't work that way. Between the two of us, I'm the only one in a condition to get myself organized, to keep things running. If I was a little less sure on my feet, the situation would be very different. Then we'd both be dependent on someone else's assistance. And would I find myself turning into an Edwin, then? Would I make the same demands of the person taking care of me? My knees click when I walk. Now and then I have pains in my chest when I wake up in the morning and get out of bed. I don't really have any other complaints at the moment—but I still don't know how long I can keep going like this. If Edwin takes a sudden turn for the worse, so will I. For every year that goes by, we both get just as old. I don't know. It would really be a good idea to have someone else here. Regardless of what happens with Edwin, I won't be able to cope all by myself. I've thought about renting out Edwin's old room. It's been empty a long time. I just don't have enough suitable things to furnish it with. His bed is still there and the dresser with the mirror. That's all. But it would be simple for a lodger to move in. They could use the kitchen and bathroom as much as they wanted. We would have to work out some suitable arrangement. It would have to be a man who rents the room, I think. There's a better chance of reaching an understanding with a man—you never know what's going on with women. Single men, however, often live fairly uneventful lives. A student, maybe, or a commuter from out of town, someone who just needs a room for the working week, who doesn't need any more space than is absolutely necessary to relax, eat, and sleep. I wouldn't be against introducing the kind of comfortable day-to-day relationship that might come out of such an arrangement—nor the extra money that would come along with it—into our lives. And if there were someone else here, then I'd have some support in case things became really serious with Edwin—obviously, our boarder wouldn't be under any obligation to assist us, but in any case, having another man around the house would still be a kind of relief. It would be enough to know that I wasn't alone, that there was someone else here I could depend on. I'd feel secure in the knowledge that he was nearby.

I gave Edwin a little to drink, but most of it came up again. Like it had boiled in his mouth.

"Erna," he said.

Yes, I replied.

"Have I been a good husband to you?"

I responded that he had, of course.

He thought for a moment, and then he asked, as though trying to persuade me, "You think I've been a bad husband, don't you?"

No, I answered, I didn't think that.

He snorted. "But how is that possible? How can you manage to avoid feeling an intense dislike for me, given my condition?

I'm a bad husband, I am. Even I know it. How can you not think so too?"

"But I don't think so," I said. "I don't think that you're bad."

"But I am. Look at me. Look at me, goddamn it! Look at me!"

He almost screamed the last "look at me." He opened his mouth then and grimaced—trying to make himself look as ugly as he possibly could—gnashing his teeth, rolling his eyes, and sticking out his tongue.

"Look at me, you bitch!" His tongue had gone back into his mouth so that he could shout again, at the top of his lungs: "Look at me! Don't you think I've been a bad husband?"

He made his mouth into an oval and clicked his tongue around repulsively. "Answer me! And be honest! Don't you think I'm awful?"

"No," I answered firmly. I felt something that must have been anger, and it made my tongue stiff when I spoke. "No, I don't think you're awful."

"You goddamned bitch!" he screamed. "Standing there lying right to my face! What makes you think I'll ever believe another one of your fucking lies? Have you ever given me an honest answer about anything? Have you? Answer me, damn it! Have you?"

I knew that if I said anything I would regret it immediately. He shifted himself around in the rocking chair.

Now he asked, "Do you think I'm a good person?" I didn't answer. I didn't want to get pulled into one of his endless arguments any more than I already had.

"Do you think I'm a good person?" he repeated. I needed to wash my hands. I had been standing there and rubbing them together this entire time, without thinking. Now my palms were pale and sweaty.

"Answer me, you bitch!" He was getting himself worked up again. "Do you think I'm a good person or not? Can't you answer a simple question? You were doing fine a minute ago!"

I didn't answer. I wanted to leave, but I couldn't get myself to move.

"Erna?" he asked, but I couldn't make myself reply, not when he was behaving like that. Finally I told him that we'd talk more about it after he calmed down a bit. I began to walk toward the door, and the gum wrappers parted before me like a swarm of live things.

"Erna?" he repeated. There was something utterly devastated in his voice that I just couldn't turn my back on. So I stopped with my hand on the doorknob.

"Erna?"

I didn't know what to say.

"I think I'm getting very near the end," he said. The last words seemed to bubble up from his throat. His voice was unfamiliar. It gurgled up from his chest. He started to say something else, but stopped to clear his throat. He hawked repeatedly. Like there was something he was trying to cough up. And then, something came up. I thought at first that it was chewing gum, but it looked like a tide of white larva. They slid right out of his mouth, over his lips, and disappeared into his beard. He turned his face toward me and gagged. I felt sorry for him. It looked like he couldn't breathe, and whatever word he was trying to say had stuck in his throat on its way up. Perhaps it was my name. I thought of my name being stuck inside his throat. He stretched his shaking hand out toward the dresser and grabbed the box with those all-important pills in it, then shook out some white pieces of gum, and tossed it all into his mouth, trembling.

"Erna!" he shouted, with his mouth full, so suddenly that I jumped. "Erna, you have to help me." Tiny pearls of white nectar dribbled out of the corners of his mouth.

He held up a hand—hoping of course I would take it in mine—but I wasn't sure what I was seeing, so I didn't answer.

"Erna!" he whined. He sounded like he'd just woken up from a bad dream, still half-asleep.

"You have to help me!" he whimpered. "For the love of God!"

If he was acting, it was a very convincing performance. Like fear was choking the life out of him.

"Erna! Help me! I don't remember how I look. I've forgotten. I've forgotten how I look!"

But I was looking at him. He shook his head and gasped.

"Erna! Please, Erna!"

I had no idea what I should say to him. There was something genuine about this routine, and it moved me. I told myself that it didn't matter whether it was real or another game. I looked at him again—his head looked like it was covered with mold, probably psoriasis, which had entered a new and advanced phase—but when I leaned closer to him, I saw that his forehead was covered with small, fine hairs, a down almost, like the first growth of something new, fresh, and wild. I described it to him, the hairs, but didn't say anything about the scabs. They hung loosely, most of them, pierced by the small white hairs, ready to be plucked out. I described his ears to him, which are like conch shells in his hair. He asked what color it was, his hair, and I answered white. His earlobes are round and thick, they look kind of like candies—I told him that, and he laughed. His nose—and I almost jumped, looking at it so closely, I don't know if I'd ever noticed how big it was, how prominent—is just a confused mass of flesh on the tightly stretched skin of his face, as though entirely too much flesh had been allotted to it. There's a deep furrow between his eyes, just like his face had been divided into separate parts, and I said that this was what gave him such a serious expression. No man with a forehead like that can ever look cheerful. He smiled, and a dark shadow appeared in his beard—I felt my heart pound—as though a new mouth was opening there.

"And my eyes?" he asked. I looked at his eyes. The pupils are empty, like pinholes, but I didn't mention this. I talked around it by mentioning some other quality of his face. He lifted his hand again and held it out until I put mine in it, but that was a mistake, I should never have given him my hand. I thought he just wanted to thank me, but once he got hold of me, he wouldn't let go. "And what about my eyes?" he asked again, and it felt like my hand was in a vice. He stared right at me and squeezed my hand even harder. I tried to twist it free, but he went on squeezing. I screamed at him to let go, and felt my ring biting into my knuckles.

Eventually he did let go. My fingers unfolded like a flower. Edwin's head sank down to his chest. He closed his eyes. It looked like he was ashamed of himself, or at least that's what I hoped. I didn't say anything—there was no point in reprimanding him. I just stood there a while, at a safe distance, watching him. I wanted him to know that I was standing there thinking about him. I massaged my fingers. There were deep marks in them from my ring. Edwin doesn't wear his ring anymore. Impossible to get it on with all the weight he's put on since he started living in his rocking chair. He must have gained forty pounds at least. His legs have swelled up so much they look like little tree stumps. They're covered with red marks, and his skin is cracked all over, as though it's become too tight to hold him in. He never courted me. We just got married. That was that.

I'D BE PERFECTLY happy to have my legs removed, they're only in the way, they could be frostbitten for all I know, everything below the knees, or maybe starting just above them, either way, I could have them amputated without risking anything, presumably I wouldn't even notice the difference, and if I did, it would undoubtedly be for the better, since with my legs out of the picture, I'd be free of unnecessary ballast . . .

I could also manage quite well without my arms, I don't use them very often in any case, it'd be just as simple to ask Sweetie to stuff some chewing gum into my face whenever she had a spare moment, everything would be easier and more practical. Sweetie, poor thing, would have an easier job of keeping me clean, too, if I didn't have arms or legs, she'd be able to wash me as easily as she washes all her knickknacks, she could just wipe me down with a cloth and she wouldn't have to be afraid of me grabbing her either, which she said she doesn't like, naturally, she'd know where I stood, so to speak, and I'd finally be just where she wanted me . . .

Anyway, I would still be who I am, my personality isn't in my hands or my feet, I'm sure of that now, if there was ever any doubt, so everything would be the same, except that I'd be propped up with a pillow and strapped in, just a huge larva sitting here in my chair . . .

They might as well cut off my ears too, the silence would be a blessing, and while they're at it, they should take my nose too, all I really need is a hole to breathe through, losing my sense of smell would be a liberation, smell is the most obstinate of all our senses, it's impossible to get the upper hand with your smell . . . and the worst smell of all is Sweetie's bathroom stink, in fact I've long suspected that she does it on purpose, that she sits on the toilet an extra long time before pushing out her business so that the smell will have a chance to spread itself through the whole of the room. And there have never been any sounds, just a few dull splashes, like someone is emptying out the leftovers from dinner, and when she's gone there's never any of the usual shit smell lingering, just that sour odor of hers that spreads like a heat wave through my little sanctum . . .

They're welcome to remove my eyes, it would be just like having a tumor cut out, that's what they are, my eyes, tumors, after all, they're just in the way . . .

My mouth is about the only thing that I want to keep, it's pretty difficult to imagine myself without a mouth, since I have to have something to open so I can drink and have a little solid food when it's necessary, and then, last but not least, to call Sweetie with, every hour of the day, which is the only fun I can still have. I'd let them take my teeth, if they wanted, but that's all . . .

And really, once they get going, I'd tell them they might as well take away my ass and whatever's left of my thighs, the stumps down there. I'm quite certain they could take all of that away and still leave me, the real me, the core of my being, intact . . . I would be just like I am today, exactly the same, even after most of me was removed, provided that the procedure is carried out by people who actually know what they're doing. Take it away! I'd cope quite well if I lost everything from my chin down. I could still chew my gum, so what's the difference, in the end . . .

They even could set fire to me if they wanted to, burning away whatever's left, and if my skull could tolerate the heat, then why not throw it in too, I'd still be sitting there when the smoke cleared, exactly the same as I am now, and I'd probably be a much better person for it, free of all my physical afflictions, my brain secure within the vault of my skull, able to listen to all the worst stories of sickness, decay, and decline with nothing but equanimity and peace of mind, finally able to use all of my time to rest, I'd be thrilled, never saying anything, but really thrilled, I'd never stop smiling . . .

It'd be a disappointment for the worms . . . but all the better . . . I'd love to know I wasn't leaving any food over for them . . . the last bunch of board members we have to deal with on earth . . . no my friends, you get nothing from me but a pile of dry bones . . . I think about death too often, that much I'm sure of, no one needs to tell me that. But I can't help it. It's like a vipers' nest up here, like a bunch of maggots . . . What happens to your head when life is finally over? Sooner or later the soil gets in, it works its way into your eyes and upwards to the holy of holies . . . Then the worms throw themselves onto the main course . . . Afterwards, they're teeming with my thoughts, full of my experiences, and thanks to them, I can live on eternally, beneath the ground . . . yes, they'll spread me through the endless darkness for eternity . . . I'd be happy if I could sit here all concentrated into one little piece, but it's not as easy as I think to ignore the rest of me, despite the state it's in . . . some of the wiring still works, so I can't be finished with my body so easily . . . yes, some of the threads are still hanging here and there, there are more connections than I thought, for instance I still get thirsty at the thought of a mug of flat Coca-Cola . . .

Mr. Reum had surgery on his back once and the incisions never properly closed up again, they'd opened him up from his shoulders all the way down to his heels, but sewing him together again apparently didn't go too well, though it wasn't entirely their fault, his skin just wouldn't cooperate, frankly, the lips of his wound curled away from each other like magnets with opposing poles . . . instead of healing they just formed a permanent rubbery crust on either shore . . .

We tried to get a settlement from the hospital that was responsible for that debacle, but we never got anywhere with them . . . After that, we asked the authorities about some form of compensation, but didn't get anywhere with them . . . Reum just had to adjust to living with his lovely little attraction . . . Our younger staff members even started calling it the Grand Canyon . . . After a while, taking a trip to the Grand Canyon became an expression most of us used without even thinking . . .

Those were the kinds of duties we assigned to the younger members of the staff, they didn't have any say in the matter, they had to take on all the really thankless work. But they benefited from it. Washing old men between their legs has a calming effect on you during that time of life, when your glands are most active, and I'm sure that we helped a number of young women avoid unwanted pregnancies by way of the modest distribution of these unpleasant chores at the institution. The board should have commended us for our farsightedness. Usually the nurses who got these assignments were the daughters of board members . . . Moreover, it was surprising how capable they were, most of them, after nothing more than three-week course in practical nursing, standing there in their green capes and little caps, which always made me think of the girls who used to sell confections, their faces serious so as to show us they were ready to start their careers . . . all we needed to do was snap our fingers and they took on any task with honor . . . I can never be rid of them . . .

. . . I still hear them, all of them, I hear their steps, the clip-clop of the head nurses shoes . . . the clicking of the girls' wooden

soles . . . the endless shuffling of the old folks' slippers . . . it's just
not possible to tell the difference between a man and a woman
based on the sounds of their shuffling . . . no, it's always the same
kind of scraping sound from all of them, a miserable whispering
chorus filling our white hallways with the song of death . . . I
hear them whispering to me that they might as well be allowed
to die as continue this meaningless wandering, from nothingness
to nothingness . . .

What can I do? I always felt like I was lying to their faces whenever
I said good morning to them. How did I ever manage to have
a normal conversation with any of them? I did the best I could.
Or did I? Christ! Handing out rationalizations was the only real
service I was able to provide up there. I rationalized the glaring
lack of equipment and personnel, I rationalized the residents'
illnesses, I rationalized the worst of their symptoms, I rationalized
the doctor's discouraging prognoses, and I even rationalized
death. Every single day, I turned it away, like an uninvited guest.
I rationalized the improper behavior of our patients' relatives, the
ones who'd heard there might be an inheritance waiting, I excused
them and explained away their greed, saying they didn't know
any better, despite the fact that you could see the dollar signs in
their eyes from a mile away . . .

This will go just fine, I said to Mrs. Pedersen. She'd only been
there a couple of days and was scared out of her wits. She clamped
onto her bed like a limpet. Really, this will all go just fine, there's
nothing to worry about, all of us need a little time to get used to
a new environment. It's a little scary to begin with, but everyone
here does just fine after a while. I glanced over at the other bed,
still sitting and holding Mrs. Pedersen's hand, but there was Mrs.
Lund, who was propped up on her pillows and eating straw-
berries with her fingers, which were black with age. She rustled
her hands in the green basket, they were like charred wood, and
it was clearly and completely repulsive, completely intolerable,

the sight of these black, fumbling fingers in among those red berries, so much so that I had to swallow several times to make sure I didn't vomit . . .

Rest assured, I'll ask death not to pull any punches when he comes for me . . .

I'd prefer cremation, when the time comes, just to be on the safe side, though I think I may have forgotten to mention this to Sweetie, I'd better remember to let her know the next time she comes in, I have to make it clear that I want to be cremated, and she'd better promise me to take care of it, arrange it with the attorney, put it in my will that I want them to turn the heat up all the way, no half measures, I want to be entirely incinerated, I want there to be nothing left of me . . .

It won't be enough for my life to be peeled off of me like a glove from a shrunken hand, no, I'll only be convinced that I won't be dragged back here after I've been entirely reduced to ashes. As long as that's taken care of, I'll have no anxiety about anything, I'll just be ashes, spread by the winds . . . They can scatter me over the waves of the ocean, or empty me into the toilet . . . I don't care. It's up to them . . .

Then again, hell, if it really hurts and goes on hurting, like this burning in my throat and stomach, if that's the way it'll be when I die, then I have nothing against postponing it a little bit longer . . . unless I can get it over with all at once . . . Fuck, I'd rather go on sitting here in peace and sleeping like usual than be tormented by death over the course of a week or so . . .

And if it seems like it's taking too long, I'll call out to Sweetie and give her the order, get her to put an end to it, that's the reason I still keep her around, to help out in case death isn't as easy as I hope it'll be . . . I've seen several cases where death drags on and on . . . I just need to shout to her and she'll come running, it's no more than she owes me after a whole life together, a life that's

taken forever to get through, and she's sworn to me, sworn that she'll do it, that she'll finish me off if I start slipping. I only need to pretend that I have a screw loose and she'll come rushing in to wrap things up, because that's what she promised me, she took a solemn oath. Yes, Mr. Death, we'll take the inside curve and beat you to the finish line . . . I'd rather get a bullet in the head than sit here for days and days, wasting away slowly . . . Hear that? No mercy, please . . . I don't want there to be anything left . . . Take it all, I mean it, don't leave so much as a bedroom slipper behind, annihilate me, smash me into kindling, into dust, then vacuum me up, leave no evidence, I don't want to be remembered for anything. I just want it to be over, you win either way, so please do me this favor . . . I long for you to come and beat my thoughts into submission . . . they've plagued me long enough, do nothing but torment me, are incapable of doing anything besides torment me . . . all they think about, all they remember, is themselves . . . But I don't want to think about them anymore . . . letting them have their way with me is a worse defeat than death . . . That's the gift you come with . . . you let us all stop worrying . . . There, I'm calming down a little, I understand, I know you're not as bad as people say, I just have to talk to you like a reasonable man, the only people who fear you are the ones who still hope to get something out of you, to use you for their own ends, I've always known that, always had a special faith in you, undoubtedly you'll take the time to listen to a poor old man, since you've already taken the time to put your hand on his shoulder . . .
Has it been there long?
I've always known that you were near. But this is something else. The act of dying, rather than just knowing that you're going to die . . .
You were here, waiting, when I came into the bathroom . . .
I recognized you at once . . . I'd seen you many times before, up at Kronsæther . . .

I fooled you with one of them, Mr. Fredriksen with the horse face, who swallowed something or other wrong and began to croak like a frog during dinner. I'd just meant to stop by his room to wish him a happy Easter on my way out that night, but I got a real shock when I saw him there, lurched in his chair, that old bastard, his face turning blue. I took hold of his jaw with one hand, his skin felt like the rind on a dry orange, and then I forced open his mouth and stuck my other hand into it, wiggling and wiggling it until finally the whole thing was inside. His swallowing reflex helped it down into his esophagus, and for a moment I was afraid my entire arm would end up down his throat, but then everything stopped, I wasn't able to go any further. When I stretched out my middle finger, I felt something wet, something that moved when I pressed against it. I began to get sick to my stomach. It was like something deep inside him was still alive, something that the dehydration hadn't reached yet. Then I felt something else, something slick and hard lodged in there pretty tight, so I got my fingertips around it and pulled. I felt it budge, but it wouldn't come free . . . it was almost like it had barbs holding it in place. I decided to risk using force and pulled with all of my strength, trying to tear the thing out, now feeling like I was a plumber clearing an obstruction out of a sewage pipe . . . and the shit I was pulling at was so hard I could believe it had been building up for years. The most embarrassing thing was when I realized I wouldn't be able to get my hand free without help . . . Fredriksen's throat was like a suction pump, thanks to the dryness. I had to call one of the nurses to help me get loose . . . She got a good grip on his head while I pulled, and then there was a pop like a cork coming out of a bottle and I was loose again, with the rest of his dinner following, spilling out into the air, but I was more interested in studying what I was holding between my fingers, a chicken wing, in fact, with a broken bone, gnawed almost clean, but not completely. I helped the nurse stabilize his breathing, which meant pounding that fucker from every side until we heard him gasp, which told us that his air passages were open again. She looked at me but said nothing, obviously shaken up about all this, though I'm not sure if it was me or that old son of a bitch Fredriksen who struck her as being most repugnant just then, but what does it matter, she would have been right either way. It turned out fine, Fredriksen was used to rough treatment, he had to be kick-started like an old motor every morning anyway, his lungs would seize right up if he didn't get a few good wake-up smacks on his back and chest, and when the worst of his coughing had passed, he always took his assailants by the hand and thanked them . . .

I dreamed about them at night, especially in the beginning, what else could you expect. I saw hundreds of them, packed cheek by jowl up under the roof, because in my dreams, they were always angels, a billowing flock of silent angels, every one with wings, fluttering softly, arrayed in two lines in mid-air, staring down at us mortals with a kind of patronizing tolerance . . .

I think that it was the dreams that helped me to go on, they instilled those miserable creatures at Kronsæther with a kind of value, and me with a kind of respect for them. I labored under the delusion that they were still worth something, and this helped me to treat them better than I would have otherwise, if I despised them, for instance, or even felt sympathy for them. In fact, in a way, I felt inferior to them, since I'd never experienced anything like their pitiful helplessness or the degradations of their rigidly controlled and closely monitored daily routines . . .

Those people had no other choice than to find peace in whatever way they could, willingly allowing themselves to be raised up in some truly ghastly contraptions, happy just to have the shit removed from their bodies. For them, dignity was a quaint, out-dated notion, nothing more than a word, the letters hard and matter-of-fact as fossils, hard like the desiccated little pellets that came out of them and that made them scream like they were being torn apart . . . If it had been up to me, they would all have been smothered in their beds on their first night there . . .

I'M WORRIED ABOUT him. He doesn't feel like eating anymore. He sits there and pokes at his food like a child, pushes his plate away, won't look at it. I had to throw away everything I made for him this last week. It used to be so easy. He never used to be fussy about food. At least not as long as he got what he wanted. He'd sit like a baby bird when I brought his food to him, stretching his head forward on his neck and opening his mouth wide. I put the plate in his lap, cut up his meatballs, and fed them to him. I could see them slide down his throat when he swallowed. I usually blew on every bite, if the meat was still too hot, but one day he protested, said that I was getting germs on his food—and then he got really worked up and announced that from then on he would feed himself. He made a mess like a pig, of course, but didn't worry about it, or notice it. It just disappeared and was gone, as far as he was concerned. I couldn't stand to look at him. I had to leave the room when he ate. Otherwise I wouldn't have been able to keep from saying something.

Whenever he was finished with dinner, I took a handful of yellow or green Orbit—they look like teeth—and fed him his gum from my cupped hand. God knows how many packs he's chewed through over the years—possibly even several thousand.

I should have been keeping track of the expense from the first pack onward, from the time I bought him the first one. Then I could throw my calculations down onto the table and tell him how much his enormous appetite for the stuff has cost us.

If he goes on like this, I'll have to do something. But what? I need to get something nourishing into him. It's so difficult to know what he needs when he refuses to say anything. He complains all the time, but rarely mentions anything specific. Maybe there's something he would really like that I could give him every day and which would build his strength up, but which he hasn't mentioned because he doesn't know he needs it. Maybe there's something that would change him after just a few spoonfuls, change his outlook and bring back his appetite. I should talk to someone. But who? It's been a long time since Dr. Amonsen moved away. I didn't dare tell Edwin. He's always seen Dr. Amonsen as his savior. His faithful defender. Edwin's always had complete faith in him. I think he believes Dr. Amonsen could help him with just about anything. But Dr. Amonsen isn't here anymore. I haven't found anyone else. I don't even know if Edwin would want someone else. I might not like it either, if I found him a new doctor. There was something unique about Amonsen. He would be hard to replace. I've always lied to Edwin when he asked about Amonsen. I didn't know what else I could do. I've worked to embellish my story and make it more believable. When Edwin asks me to ask Dr. Amonsen about something, I always let a couple of days go by before I tell him what Amonsen's reply was. And as long as I say it was Amonsen who told me this or that, Edwin accepts it immediately. As far as Edwin's concerned, the doctor's word is still law—to such a degree that I've been tempted to use his name as an all-purpose motivator. I've often been on the verge of saying that I've spoken to Dr. Amonsen about something or other, and that he said so and so on the subject . . . But I can't do it too often. For all I know, Edwin sees right through me. But now I'm wondering whether I should consider it an act of mercy to invoke the doctor's name. I could give Edwin strict instructions from Dr. Amonsen to get some nourishment into himself, regardless of whether or not he feels like eating. The doctor did tell me, when I spoke with him last, that things would become critical very quickly if Edwin didn't eat . . . It's almost like life itself is the only thing still keeping him alive. Is this the end, then? Is that what's happening? Is Edwin planning to leave me? Is he sitting there dying without saying a word, without making a sound—other than those childish outbursts of his, which don't mean anything at all? Is that why he isn't eating? Because he knows that the end is near? Because he's noticed that it's already begun?

I talked with Dr. Amonsen today, and he said that . . .

I need to get someone to come around and settle the question for me, that's obvious. Maybe take him somewhere. I can't imagine there's any other way out of this. But who would I get to do it? And where will they take him? Nothing's been arranged. Maybe I should talk to the super about it and ask him what he thinks I should do. He seemed like someone who knows how to fix things. Despite being so young. It's the sort of thing he should know. It suits his position. Repair work. He needs to know how to handle things that break down. Emergencies. Maybe if I could get him to come up here under some pretext, I could mention the situation to him. No one should have to be alone when it comes to this. We should have planned for it. A decision should have been made a long time ago, so that all the responsibility didn't fall on my shoulders now. To think that Edwin worked his whole life looking after old people, people who needed nursing . . . He of all people should have the foresight to deal with this. What else was all his hard work for? Things should have taken care of themselves . . . It should've all gone without saying . . . But instead, there he sits. Forgotten by everyone. I'll tell him Amonsen says hello . . . and that . . .

What is it I'm so frightened of? This isn't the first time he's stopped communicating. There have been many days when I wasn't able to get a single intelligible word out of him. Weeks have gone by when there's been nothing but abuse. And then the times when he just sits there and screams like a wounded animal. I shouldn't make things harder for myself than they need to be. I shouldn't worry over nothing. I should save my strength for when I really need it. Realistically, we have another year together at the most, him with me, me with him. He still knows how to rattle me. He hasn't forgotten his old tricks. That's his great talent, getting me to give in to all my fears. This hunger strike is clearly just a new way of manipulating me. He wants to see how long I'll be able to stand it before I lose my patience and start threatening him, to make him eat. And when that happens, he'll celebrate. His latest obscure little triumph. I just don't know what to think. It's obvious what's happening to his body, but no one knows anything about what's happening to his mind. I asked Dr. Amonsen about it once, what was actually wrong with Edwin. He just told me that it seemed like he'd never really recovered his full range of faculties. I asked whether or not it had anything to do with Edwin's mind, and he said that it undoubtedly did. Then I asked whether it was anything serious, but Amonsen just shrugged his shoulders noncommittally; I couldn't tell what he was thinking.

Once in a while I've even heard Edwin singing in there—humming small, happy refrains to himself—but when I'd open the door a moment later, he'd be sitting there, his eyelids trembling, whimpering, almost out of breath. I don't know what to think. It seems like making me worry is what keeps him happy. He's a monster. That's what he is, a monster. You can see it in the things he enjoys. Like an animal. Like a beast of prey. Torturing its kill before devouring it. A cunning and dangerous creature. He enjoys making me suffer, making me unsure of how to deal with him. It's his way of keeping himself at the center of my attention. He knows that once I start worrying about him, he never leaves my thoughts. My fear grows out of my conscience. And Edwin wants all of me. He doesn't want to share me with anyone. He'll drive me out of my mind with his little complaints, if that's what it takes. That's what he's been trying to do for years . . . But this time, I'll let him have his way. If he doesn't want to eat, I won't force him to eat. I want to see how long it takes before he becomes desperate. I've been far too nice to him. He doesn't know what real desperation is. I don't know if he's ever known. Well, I won't nag him anymore. If he doesn't want to eat, he doesn't have to eat. He'll get what he wants—which is exactly what he's used to. This time I'll wait until I hear him beg for food. He'll have to get down on his knees, so to speak. He'll have to implore me to set foot in his bathroom again.

Sometimes I think—yes, I've been almost certain of it—that his vision must have come back. I get the feeling that he's sitting there and watching me, following every little movement I make. It's something you can just feel, isn't it, when someone's watching you? It's been like that several times—that I've been quite certain he was staring at me. Yes, he can see. He just pretends that he can't. I wouldn't be surprised.

After all, what could give him better insight into all the things going on around him than pretending to be blind? It's been on my mind . . . I've been trying to remember all the things I've ever done while I was in with him, just in case there might have been something indecent, or insulting to him, that he could have seen . . . Maybe he's just waiting for the perfect moment to tell me—waiting for a day when I'm behaving just a little too freely in there. He'll look up suddenly and tell me what color my dress is—that would be just like him. Anyway, even if he really can't see very well, I've never been entirely convinced that his sight is as bad as he would have me believe. For all I know he's still able to make out my outline, at the very least—a shape in the room, almost obliterated by the light, like an apple core. And if he isn't lying, if he can't see anything at all, I wonder what that's like—just darkness, or just light? Sometimes—and this much is certain—he follows me with his gaze, turns when I walk past him, turns his head in whatever direction I'm disappearing into. I assume he's just listening to me walk away. That's what he does. He listens to every little sound he hears, or imagines he hears. I suppose his sense of hearing must be highly acute. Ever since his sight began deteriorating. They say the one compensates for the other. He hears voices from far away, complains about noises in the night, he hears insects that aren't there. He even hears things down in hell, he says. Yes, that's what he says now and then, hoping to make some kind of impression on me. It's clear his vision will never improve. There's even less chance of it returning. That would be hoping for a miracle. I see it whenever I look into his eyes. They might as well be made out of plastic. The pupils are empty, like tiny holes. Liquid seeps out of them when the temperature drops. Matter weeps from them every autumn. It looks like he's crying. Big drops of sap—just like tears, but thicker. His knuckles crack, his scalp dries out, and his hands become like claws, ice cold.

But the thought that he might recover is worse. I don't know if I can tolerate any more changes. The days have a good rhythm. It's been the same way for so long now that it's impossible for me to think that it could be different. The only thing I want is for everything to continue as it is, from now until it all stops entirely. It doesn't make any difference to Edwin. I could go in to him now and say that it was Monday morning, and then wait until Thursday or Friday to feed him—he wouldn't protest. I don't even know if he'd be able to tell he was hungrier than usual. I almost envy him, sitting there in his own little world, cut off from everything. He has no worries. He's able to let his thoughts take him wherever they want. I, on the other hand, have to do the thinking for both of us.

It's gotten colder. I'll put a ski cap on him, just in case.

I'M AFRAID THAT I'm losing my grip on things . . .
Damn it to hell . . .

I've begun belching loudly whenever Sweetie comes in here . . . I
don't mean to do it, of course, they just slip out somehow, they
just rumble up my throat like rabbits out of a hat. And I can't do
anything about it. It startles us both . . . and she drops something
in the sink, I hear it dancing around down there forever . . . She
doesn't say anything, just leaves again with offended, strident
footsteps . . . She thinks that I'm doing it just to frighten her . . .
I didn't hear her come in. Am I losing my hearing now too? That's
a new tactic of hers, something she's only begun to do recently,
let herself into the bathroom as quietly as she can, tiptoe to the
sink, and suddenly turn the faucets on all the way, the old pipes
scream when the water starts to come out and the noise scares
me out of my wits, I'm not ready for it, oh no, Sweetie hasn't
forgotten how to push my buttons, she still knows how to give
me a scare . . .

It's gotten colder, no doubt about it, Sweetie just came in and put
a ski cap on my head, it itches constantly, but I can infer from
this that it's getting colder, why else would she have put a ski cap
on my head, there must be a nip in the air. Her, all she needs to

do to check the temperature is open a window.

It's completely quiet. I itch. No, not completely quiet . . . I hear a voice, far away. Is it from a radio? Once in a while, I hear some of the neighbors through the ventilation system, though the voices are unrecognizable after their long trip through the duct work, it's like they're dead, those people, like their voices have been traveling and traveling and only now are reaching their destination . . . It makes it sound as though I'm in an enormous, echoing room, a common room like the ones we had up at Kronsæther, seven or eight meters tall . . . Presumably it's nighttime, which means that Sweetie went to bed a long time ago . . . She goes to bed so early, just like a farmer's wife . . . She's always done that . . . It's touching, the care she provides for me. What would I do without her? I feel like I should thank her, but I know that I'll never get myself to do it . . .

She's sleeping now, I can hear her snore, whimpering just like a little wounded animal, she sleeps with two duvets, she gets so cold, they rise and fall in tempo . . .

Me, I get sweaty . . . and then I freeze my ass off . . . It's like a damp, ice-cold hell in here, death's antechamber, it can take up to twenty-four hours for a wet towel to dry out in my bathroom, but this has nothing to do with the weather outside, no, it just has to do with my wife, hers is the hand that adjusts the thermostat . . . She can change winter into summer any time she likes, if she wants to . . .

Cold or warm, I don't say anything, I don't give a damn, for me the seasons have come to an end, the yearly cycles have stopped going round, time stands still, it makes no difference to me, all those changes, they go their way without me . . . though maybe I'll ask her to rub a special ointment onto my buttocks to protect them from the cold, just in case . . .

The cry of a seagull. I don't remember what that sounds like . . .

I could hear something completely different and think it was a seagull. Listen to the seagulls, I'd say, and make an absolute ass of myself . . . That new fluorescent bulb he put in, that kid, sounds different . . . Must be stronger . . . It's like a swarm of very tiny insects . . .

That fucking super . . .

That fucking bitch . . .

No one thinks about me, the one who has to sit here all the time with nothing but that goddamn buzzing in his ears . . .

This miserable fucking life! . . . hell would be preferable . . . I told her as much, today . . . in exactly those words . . . It made a real impression on her, that was obvious, because she stayed away for the rest of the day, she didn't bring my food like she usually does, and she didn't come in to ask if I was thirsty either, I could hear her banging around in the kitchen all day so I know it wasn't because she'd gone out . . . What does she do in there all day? I hear her thumping around with one thing or another, it's constant, she never takes a break, but I can't understand what it is that requires so much of her attention, so much of her time, every single day. I hear the clatter of dishes banging against each other, I think. She can't possibly have that much to wash . . . just the knives, forks, and plate I've used . . . and the silverware and plate she used herself . . .

It sounds like she's cleaning up, but there can't be all that much to clean if cleaning's all she ever does . . .

Is she busy changing the apartment around? Maybe she's replaced everything out there since I last was able to see it? If I got my sight back, would I think I was in someone else's home? But of course I can't remember what it used to look like, so maybe it would all be exactly the same but still look entirely alien to me . . . Maybe she's rearranging the rooms? Maybe she isn't ever pleased with the way things look? I would've thought she'd be too weak to move the larger things around by herself. Does that mean that someone's helping her? It seems like she's certainly sleeping well at night, which suggests that she's worn out by the time she goes to bed . . . which itself suggests that she's been keeping . . .

It's a mystery what she's been doing with herself all of these years . . .

I awaken as from slumber . . .

The telephone is ringing. The ringing gets louder day by day, with extra bells installed all over the apartment, in various rooms . . . In addition, Sweetie has small lamps here and there that are set up to flash when someone's calling . . . It's like a carnival in there . . . The only thing that is missing is a nice young friend, our super, for example, riding by her side in a brightly lit Ferris wheel . . . I have a feeling Sweetie hasn't been able to get him out of her mind since his visit . . .

That's why she keeps calling him, of course, she wants to land some young stud who can come up and keep her company, there's no shame in asking for a little company, not at her age, Sweetie is well aware of that, but really, I have a hard time seeing Sweetie in any kind of romantic light, her suspicious nature makes that impossible . . .

I make no attempt to hide the fact that I know something's going on out there. She doesn't answer me now even if I shout as loud as I can, just mumbles, or not even that, she doesn't close her mouth long enough to make words . . . it's impossible to understand her noises, not even with ears like mine. Then I recognize it, the smell of caramel, goddamn her, so that's what she's doing, at her age, what the hell is she thinking . . .

I wonder if she and Dr. Amonsen are plotting something together . . . Or maybe she's found us another doctor, one she's already won over to her side, somehow, not that she's said anything to me . . . a new doctor and already in her pocket, a doctor she can manipulate however she wants, who's making decisions about me according to her directives, who gives diagnoses according to her whims . . . I don't really believe it, but I can't rule out the possibility entirely. Sweetie's very trusting, and she gets worse every day . . . and everything she thinks she's managed to achieve without my knowing about it, everything she manages to keep me in the dark about, takes on a special significance for her . . . I hear her put the cap back onto her lipstick . . .

She does whatever she wants, she knows exactly what she can take liberties with, and I have no other choice than to put up with it, time is completely on her side . . . Is it my own fault that I have to put up with this monster, yes, this monster who comes in here and sits down to take a shit barely three feet away from me without worrying till hours later about flushing? Did I make her this way? Am I the one who did this to her? Do I only have myself to blame for everything?

I ask her: What the hell is it that you are doing, making a fool of yourself like that, you whore? But then she's gone, without making another sound, as though I've scared all life away with my sudden outburst . . .

Goddamn this hellish silence that settles over everything whenever I take the time to say something . . .

Silence is Sweetie's revenge, she can dump me into it whenever she likes, and she knows the silence bothers me, it's like being under a surgeon's lamp, it makes it impossible for me to avoid hearing my own thoughts . . .

What was that? What was that sound? Erna? Are you in here again? Erna? Is that you? Are you going to have a bath? Answer me if it's you, Sweetie . . . Say something, so I can hear that it's you . . .

Erna? Is there anyone here . . .

Hello? Is there anyone here? Dr. Amonsen? Answer me, damn you . . .

I know someone's there . . .

Answer me and stop tormenting a defenseless old man. I'm getting

ready to die, here, so I demand a last little bit of respect . . . I
won't tolerate you standing there without identifying yourself . . .
Who are you? Where are you? Come closer so I can touch you
. . . Closer . . .

For Christ's sake . . . this is more than I can take . . . I'm blind . . .
that means I can't see, you know? Would you please be so kind
as to say something . . . Please identify yourself . . . Turn on the
water at least, so I know you're here . . .

I would get up and come over to you, but I can't manage it . . . I
haven't stood on my own legs in years . . . They wouldn't support
me if I tried to stand . . .

So the onus is on you . . . you have to come closer to me . . .
come to me . . . Come over to my chair, so I can reach you with
my arms . . . It's easy for you, I'll bet there isn't anything wrong
with your legs, and not with your eyes either . . . You're the one
in control, here . . . I'm at your mercy, you understand . . . Don't
forget that I'm completely in your hands . . .

I HESITATED A bit, then opened the door. It wouldn't do to let him sit there alone too long at any one time. I expected him to make some kind of noise right away, but it was silent in there—as the grave. It was unusual, to say the least, for him to be so quiet. I stayed in the doorway without quite knowing what to do. He's almost always the one who speaks first. Things always start with him saying something to me, and then I answer. Our conversations have always worked that way. Could it be that I'd finally get to see what it was like to walk in on him, sleeping like an innocent? But he wasn't sleeping. He was sitting quietly and staring straight ahead, showing no sign that he'd heard me come in.

"I've brought you some cola," I said. I held the paper cup in front of me as if to show it to him, though I knew this was useless. He turned around then and said: "I've brought you some cola!" It gave me goose bumps. For one thing, his voice was unrecognizable, hoarse. Not only hoarse, but distorted. He was enunciating as though giving a stage performance. The first thing I thought was that I should walk away, close the door behind me, and wait a while before going back in again. But I changed my mind. The fizzing in the paper cup, as though the cola was impatient, helped me regain my composure. I went over to Edwin's chair and held the cup so that he could reach out and grab it if he wanted to. But I still kept a little distance between us, remembering what else he could grab, if I wasn't careful. I noticed I was no longer at ease around him.

"Are you thirsty?" I asked.

"Are you thirsty!" he repeated, in that same hideous voice. I'd never known it was possible for a grown man to behave like that.

"I'll put the cup on the dresser, so you can have it if you want it," I said.

His answer came at once: "I'll put it here on the dresser, so you can have it if you want it!"

I did as I said—he followed my movements with his head—then went to the toilet, pulled my panties down to my knees, hopped up, and sat down, which is what I'd really come for. The cola was just an excuse, so I'd have something to say to him when I came in. I must have coughed without thinking about it because suddenly he coughed too, loudly, mockingly. I wiped myself, went and washed my hands at the sink, looked at myself in the mirror, and pulled a little at the skin on my cheeks. I wet my fingers again and fussed with my hair a bit at the temples. It's gotten so long now that it falls into my face. It doesn't look very good. I'll ask Sigri if she can trim it the next time she's here. I spent a long time there at the sink and began to notice that I was almost feeling all right again. What had seemed so frightening a few minutes earlier now seemed quite simple to navigate. It was as though Edwin, for the first time in ages, had actually managed to give me some stability. I decided to take a hot bath—I couldn't even remember the last time I'd had one—but I changed my mind again just as quickly. It would be too much trouble. I went and opened a window instead, though I know Edwin hates that. He always said that I might as well wheel him outside and leave him in the middle of traffic. But now I felt like

I could allow myself to open the window. I let it stay open for a while and then stuck my head out and took a breath. I breathed deeply so that I could be certain he'd hear me—and he took a deep breath too—but still, not a word. I was impressed at his newfound self-control.

I closed the window. Airing out the room hadn't really helped that much. It was like having a damp, musty cloth pushed into my face when I turned back around.

"This place really needs a serious cleaning," I said. It would do him good, though he refuses to admit it.

"This place really needs a serious cleaning!" he said. There was something hopeful in his voice now. He sat there and waited for me to continue—irritated, perhaps, that I hadn't said more than I did.

"Well," I said.

"Well," he said.

I found myself wanting to tease him a little—I was feeling a kind of relief about everything, I don't know why. I wanted to see how far he was willing to go.

"Well, well," I said.

"Well, well," he said.

I coughed. He coughed.

"Oh," I said.

But then, nothing. His head swiveled around. And when he spoke again, his voice was crystal clear—it radiated from him, like the wrath of God:

"Why didn't you say anything the day I came home and told you?

I thought at first that he was talking about the day he'd been to the doctor and learned that he would go blind if he didn't have surgery. But then he said: "It didn't bother you at all, did it? Even though you knew that I was coming home from my last day as managing director at Kronsæther . . . and not just my last

day as managing director, but my last day as anything at all!"—
screaming now—"And I even told you how things were . . . I
told you then that from that day forth there was no one in the
world who would think of me as anything!"

I didn't know what to say. His last day at Kronsæther was
something I didn't feel I had the strength to go through a second
time. And there was no point in revisiting it. No one can help
Edwin work through his despair, his anger, his endless rehashing
of events. No one but Edwin himself. I can't let myself be sucked
into that again. I don't even feel sorry for him, not the way he
keeps his anger alive inside of him, like a best friend he refuses to
be parted from. And even though things do occasionally change
for the better—in terms of his life, in terms of the things that he
hates the most—he always changes around the chain of events in
his mind, adding or subtracting details, as it suits him, the better
to stay enraged. I won't even consider correcting him. He has all
the details on his side. He controls them, even now. He embroi-
ders everything with tiny little stitches and then remembers every
single length of thread. Maybe it's not so strange that he thinks
all the things he's fabricated are absolute truth—both the events
he bases on his memories and the ones that are outright fantasy.
He goes over every detail so often that everything becomes a
strange sort of memory for him, whether or not what he's so
worked up about ever actually happened. He doesn't even know
himself anymore.

He said: "They got rid of me as soon as they decided I was
redundant. I wasn't useful to them anymore, so they had me
expunged. Understand? The head research assistant removed my
name from all their records. It's like I was never there. Didn't
leave so much as a trace. They just erased me. And they all
forgot about me the very same day that I left. They did. There
isn't anyone left who even remembers I was ever there."

I answered that couldn't possibly be true. Of course they

remember him. Of course they still have his name on record. It wouldn't be possible for them to simply forget him. Especially considering the exemplary work he'd done up there. But he went on fuming about it. It seemed as though there was something else in particular he was expecting me to say.

"Is that so?" he shouted. "Tell me: How many of them have phoned here to check on me? How many of them have written to ask my advice? How many birthday cards do I get every year? How many packages, how many visitors? Has a single goddamned Kronsæther employee bothered to drop by here since the day I left?"

His tongue looked like it was swelling up in his mouth. It seemed like he was going to choke on his own poison.

"Well? Answer me! Answer me!"

"For God's sake, Edwin," I said, "why can't you just put the past behind you? Let's concentrate on the here and now. We don't really have that much time left, either of us." But this only made him more furious—he swallowed hard, trying to control himself—I guess the few words I'd managed to say had given him so much to get angry about that he didn't even know where to start. He tossed his head back and forth. It seemed like he was in great pain. He gasped and held his breath, as though he was trying to inflate himself, like a balloon. Then—he burst. His voice was high and hoarse:

"You have no idea what you're talking about! You're incapable of taking other people's feelings into account! You were so wrapped up in yourself that day that you didn't even notice what I was going through! You had no way of understanding my situation, understanding what it felt like to be seen as an idiot, worthless, helpless, a cripple, all at once, after years of respect!"

I tried again to calm him down, though I knew it wouldn't make any difference.

"They had no use for me anymore, don't you see? They couldn't use me anymore because I couldn't even see my own hand when I was about to sign a fucking piece of paper! Yes, all of a sudden, all at once, everything I'd done for them over the years had no significance whatsoever! Just like that! A moron, a charity case! But of course I would have had to explain all that to you, wouldn't I, on my last day, if I wanted any kind of sympathy!" I tried to say something, but no one can get a word in edgewise when he's like that. "No, no, no! You don't need to say anything. I've heard more than enough out of you already. Edwin, Edwin, poor Edwin, *poo-oor* Edwin! I hate your voice. I hate it. Understand?" He groaned. "Christ! What I wouldn't give to hear another voice in here, some other voice besides yours!" He seemed completely despondent, but it all rang a little false. He was overselling it. I heard it now. He was trying a little too hard.

"But I'll never get that. I'll die with your voice in my ears, won't I? The last thing I'll hear in this life will be your dry bleating, like a sheep's." He groaned again, as though in mortal agony. "I hate the sound of you. I do. I hate that goddamn shuffling of yours. I hate your fucking sniffling. I hate the smell of you. I hate that damned playacting of yours when you pretend to sympathize with me! It wasn't pity I needed, for Christ's sake! It was just a little support! Understand? Support, goddamn it! Don't you know what that is? Support! I needed support for Christ's sake!"

I left the bathroom. I took the paper cup with me when I went. I knew that if I gave it to him now, he would only throw it against the wall. It would be impossible for me to mop up after him, right now. He continued to shout. I could hear him all the way out in the living room. He screamed the same thing over and over again. A little later, I went and leaned my ear a tiny bit closer to the bathroom door. He was still going, but there was hardly any sound now. It was like some lunatic whispering to himself . . . I don't know where he finds the strength to carry on like that . . . about something that happened such a long time ago. But, then, all of his thoughts focus on the past. That's where he gets his strength from. It's all he has left. It's all he's concentrated on for years—how many? Twenty? Thirty? A hundred? He tears down and rebuilds the past every single day. Take something away, add something else. He sits there making tiny changes, day to day, one piece at a time . . . one tiny improvement after another, as though, some day, he might be able to put the finishing touches to his great work . . . as though, one day, everything will be complete, and he'll be able to turn around and dazzle the world with the grandeur of his creation.

M Y EARS ITCH. It's spring. It must be. I have an old frostbite wound on one of my earlobes that starts bothering me again every single spring. I want it all to be over soon . . .

My head itches, it's Sweetie's goddamn ski cap, she put it on my head just to irritate me. My throat is scratchy too. It feels like I might cough something up at any moment . . .

I reach out my arm, but don't feel anything there . . . There's a pressure in my chest, and for a moment I think the dresser's gone, but then I whack the corner of it with my hand, goddamn it . . . but now I remember it makes no difference anyway, I can't feel anything, and I can show my new wound off to Sweetie when she comes in again . . . Soon my hand is exploring the surface of the dresser . . . I wrap my fingers around a package, cold and slippery as a piece of ice . . .

I have to fumble around a little before I manage to open it, but finally I tear it to shreds, I feel it open into my lap, and the pellets of gum spill out everywhere, but I manage to catch two of them before they disappear, I take great care to get them securely into the palm of my hand and then open my mouth wide before I lift my hand up and toss them in . . . Three pellets . . . not bad for a pack of eight or ten . . . I never remember how many come in a pack . . .

My intestines are boiling. It feels like the filth inside me wants out, the little bit that there is. But which way will it go? It's not easy to predict. I thought that if I stopped eating I would also stop shitting . . . You'd almost think I was taking penicillin . . . Is this how death comes? Not from the heart, but from the intestines and then up through the throat?

I feel like I could burp continuously for at least a quarter of an hour . . .

Suddenly I hear her, she's already in here, standing over by the sink, rooting around through the shelves in the cabinet, once again she's managed to slip by me without my noticing her. What the hell's happening to me? I open my mouth to say something, but can't get a word out . . . I just cough and hack, and finally after about twenty coughs I manage to speak, I manage to make this hoarse sound I've never heard coming out of me before, it sounds like there's rusty metal being scraped around the inside of my mouth . . .

I tell her that I think the end is near for me. She doesn't hear me, or anyway doesn't answer, it's almost like she's standing somewhere farther away than usual, as though the sounds I'm making are taking a longer time to reach her. She's putting on make-up again, though it really hasn't been that long since she was here last . . . or has it? I keep thinking I can hear her taking stoppers out of bottles, various latches or caps snapping into or out of place on the glass shelves . . .

I sit here, stock-still, quiet as a church mouse, listening, waiting for just the right moment to grab hold of her . . .

The brush in her hair . . .

The hiss from her hair spray . . .

The cabinet doors banging . . .

The awful rubbing and smacking of her hands as she washes them . . . And then, a few seconds later, I lash out sideways with my arm and grab hold of her dress, hard, pulling her over to my chair . . .

She doesn't protest, like an obedient dog, though she's impatient to get this over with and move on to whatever else she has planned. I can tell that much even though the scent of her hair spray works like a sedative on me . . .

I tell her again that I think my time is about up, then I ask her to put a few things in order for me . . . I ask her to consider it my last request . . .

I've never heard her get so upset. Control yourself, for Christ's sake . . . the end is coming, and I want to touch you . . . you know it bothers me to have to be more explicit about that sort of thing . . . But her voice still has that frightened tone to it, and I understand that she won't comply with my wishes, not under any circumstances, despite the fact that she knows I'm dying . . . We don't need to make a big production of it. . . Just so long as I know that you understand that I want to touch you, to feel you . . . But suddenly it becomes clear that she's misunderstood . . . I notice it in the way she's resisting me . . .

I understand that I've embarrassed her . . . she has, almost instinctively, chosen to adopt a highly moral attitude . . . She thinks that I want her to behave immodestly . . . Goddamn her . . . Even now she won't show me the least consideration . . .

What do you say, woman? Isn't it about time that we stop kidding around? For a dying man's sake? But she's completely beside herself, twisting and tugging at her dress like a child having a tantrum . . .

Come on! Time's flying! Yes, time is rushing by . . . it's gone out to run some errands, but it'll be back for us before long . . . I'm getting angrier and angrier . . . It's amazing, all the problems she can make out of nothing, out of a simple request on my part . . . But what's happening now? God, I can taste it . . . it's coming all the way up to my mouth . . . Am I blocked up down there? It's coming. I can feel it. It's on the way up through my throat. I can't stop it. What should I do with it? Should I spit it out, or

should I try to hold it in . . .
I have to scream at Sweetie . . . If I don't, I'll choke . . .
Erna! Jesus Christ! Erna . . .

Then I remember that she's here, I have her right here, goddamn
it, I'm sitting here and holding her by the arm . . .
I continue right where I left off . . . Well, what's it going to be?
Maybe I'm exaggerating my desperation a bit, but I thought that
I'd permit myself a little affectation given how serious my situation is . . . But she won't budge, my saintly little wife . . . guarding
her compromised virtue as though it were useful for anything . . .
I don't care, my words have had the effect I expected, and I feel
calmer now. In any case, I've gained some ground . . .
Now I crane my neck forward and gape at her with my mouth
open wide, she can't deny me a bit of chewing gum, I click my
teeth together impatiently and right after that get a handful of
pellets tossed down my gullet, Sweetie's emptied an entire package
into me . . . For a moment, it's like my mouth is filled with teeth,
they burn like ice against my gums, I gasp several times before I
get control of the huge, sticky wad in my mouth . . .
I wait until I've chewed the flavor out of it entirely, then I let
Sweetie go, I tell her to go to hell . . . From now on, I'd rather
be alone . . .

When I said all that, my voice didn't sound nearly as frail as I
was afraid it would . . . I haven't burped in a long time either,
but maybe that's not such a good sign . . . I sure do fart though,
even though I haven't eaten anything in three or four days, maybe
more . . .
My chair is stuck. It was like that when I woke up. I've tried to
rock a little, but it won't budge . . . It's stuck in all the old chewing
gum on the floor, I'll bet . . . it's getting colder, which makes the
gum stiffen up. Hardened chewing gum is like concrete. I'll have to

ask Sweetie if she can rock me loose when she comes in next . . .
My lips are like paper. It feels like I'm about to catch a cold or
something. I've asked Sweetie to rub camphor into my feet, but
she says that she can't find any in the house . . . So I asked her
if she'd ask Sigri to buy some, just so we have it around, but she
snorted at me, scornfully. Superstition, she said. Superstition,
pure and simple . . .
I'm not sure whether it would help now anyway since there's
no feeling left in my feet . . . I have no feeling left in my feet . . .
I assume you have to be able to feel the camphor for it to have
any effect . . .
There is someone else out there. A voice I can't remember hearing
before. What's going on with Sweetie during the day? Is she trying
to make some new acquaintances? Does she really think this is
the right time for that?
It's hard to make out the words . . . I can hear voices, but I can't
hear what they're saying . . .
I can hear that there's someone out there, but not who it is . . .
It's a man . . .
It's not Dr. Amonsen, no, there's no mistaking his deep, resonant
voice . . .
I could yell out to her . . .
I'm sure she wouldn't tell me who it is, but at least I'd interrupt
them, her and the new guy, and if it really is a new guy, at least
he'll learn a little something . . . for instance that there's another
person living here . . .
But I'm afraid to shout. Who knows what might come out of
me . . .
Now I'm burping again . . . I have the feeling there's something
rotting deep down inside of me . . . It's like I'm burping up things
I ate years and years ago . . .
If I had the strength to do it, I'd pound on the floor tiles with
something . . . I should have a stick or a metal pole in here that

I could use to get people's attention . . .

Now it's quiet. Did he leave? Have both of them left? Or are they in the middle of something out there? It's much better to hear voices than complete silence. Silence is always the worst. Unless my ears deceive me. Am I going to lose my hearing just like I lost my sight? Is my entire body going to fail me one bit at a time?

Now there's a sound, I hear a strange sound, some gurgling, like when the air escapes from the neck of a bottle, or some other narrow space . . . And after that, a trembling, rustling vibration, followed by a new gurgling . . . And then it's absolutely quiet for a moment, almost completely still . . . Then, a new gurgling, and the vibration again, until it's drowned out by another loud gurgling . . . I'm afraid to listen too closely. I won't say anything about it when Sweetie comes next to bring my plate of meatballs and leave it in my lap . . . Everything will be like it always is when she hands me that ice-cold silverware . . . Sweetie never alters her routine, even though she knows I won't be able to swallow a single bite . . .

I remember that Sweetie's meatballs look like small, naked animals . . . I let my fingers glide over them as they lie on the plate . . . They're barely even warm. It feels like they have tiny legs on them, tiny heads. And in a sense, they do.

HE KEEPS REPEATING it over and over again, all day, loudly, almost hysterically, like it's something he's afraid he'll forget. When I put my ear to his door this morning, I heard him say, "Edwin Mortens!" At first I almost thought it wasn't him . . . like there was someone else sitting in there, shouting at him, shouting his name, hoping Edwin Mortens would show up . . . His voice has changed—I can hear that clearly now—it's getting higher-pitched and weaker with each passing day. I can barely recognize it as his . . . unless it's just me . . . it's not really possible to say. There's so much about him that's different now, so much that's disappeared and so much that's new. Is it really possible that the bathroom lights have burned out again already? I didn't think it had been all that long since the super replaced them, but when I go in, it's completely dark, and then they blink two or three times, then they're on for a moment, and then it's dark again. It's always like that. The super must have used cheap bulbs. The old ones we had lasted almost a year at a time. Or are they burning out because Edwin's getting ready to make his departure? Is that it? There was blood in his stool the other day. I mentioned it to him while I was brushing my teeth. He didn't react. It was like he hadn't heard what I'd said. He just sat there

like he was asleep. He wasn't asleep. He sighed heavily. Like
someone was tugging at him, trying to get him to stand up. He
hasn't touched his food either. For five days in a row now I've
taken away his plate, untouched, exactly as it was when I first
brought it in to him. I tried to talk to him when I went in there
with his dinner today. I explained that he needs to eat if he wants
to survive until the end of the week. But I stopped in the middle
of my lecture. It felt completely pointless to stand there like that
and talk at him. It was like a disco in there anyway. He was there,
then he wasn't there, then he was there again. The only thing
he asks for is cola. Even the packages of chewing gum on top of
the dresser sit untouched. I heard him whisper something, but
I had to bend over to understand what he was saying. I have no
idea whether his voice is really giving out or whether this is just
another affectation he's decided to try on in order to increase the
drama of the situation. Suddenly, he lifted his arm. His hand just
hung there like a dead octopus in the flickering dark. It brushed
against me, but he didn't notice.

I finally decided to call the super. The bathroom light has to
be changed. It's impossible, the way things are. I'm afraid to even
set foot in there, I find. It's like an entirely different world. Just
to be on the safe side, though, I also got out our old microwave
oven, which has been broken for years. It was sitting behind some
of Edwin's boxes in the closet. I thought it might seem odd to
the super if I only called about the light again. Especially since
he probably thinks of it as a job he's already taken care of. But
if I can get him up here to look at the oven, there wouldn't be
anything strange about mentioning the light to him too. Having
him up here again will be encouraging for me. I've found myself
looking forward to it, ever since I made up my mind to call. He
was willing to sit somewhat near to me the last time he was here,
that young man. Yes, it gave me courage. It gave me hope. The
bright, powerful light he installed in the bathroom was emblematic

of all he represented. I even plugged the old microwave oven into the outlet in the kitchen, so everything would look genuine. I'd thought of everything. The super answered the telephone just like he did the last time, after one ring, but he sounded irritable now, as though I'd disturbed him in the middle of something important. I told him about the microwave oven. He told me that he had so much to do at the moment that it wouldn't be possible for him to look at it right away. I replied that there was no hurry, it would be fine if he just came by in a few days, whenever it was convenient for him. He spoke much more quietly than he had the last time, and I found it difficult to make out some of what he was saying. Finally he said that I should give him a call in a couple of days, to remind him. Then he would see if he had a spare hour.

He'd caught me off guard. So much so that I didn't know what to believe, hanging up the phone. I had thought I was reasonably well prepared, but not for this, not in any way. He was like a different person. It made me anxious. I could hardly believe it was the same man I'd spoken to previously. I didn't know what to do. I unplugged the broken microwave oven just in case it might be dangerous to leave it as it was. But should I put it back in the closet? Now I couldn't be sure if the super would come or not. He might, for instance, find he had a spare moment between two other chores scheduled for later today. He might remember our conversation. Then, suddenly, he would show up, without any warning.

I worried about it all day long and finally decided there was no other way out than to call the super again and cancel my request, saying that it wasn't necessary anymore, that the microwave oven had begun to work again, and that I would only bother him if something else went wrong with it. Until then, he shouldn't worry about it. I wrote down what I wanted to say on a piece of paper. I found I knew his number by heart, but he wasn't home this time. There was an answering machine. It's a strange feeling to hear someone on the other end of the line and yet be unable to actually communicate with them. Finally his voice said I could leave a message after the tone, but there wasn't any tone that I was able to hear, so I just started talking. Then it beeped. And when the beep was over, I started again, but then a new beep sounded. This time I made sure to wait for a good while before I started speaking again, but then it beeped once more, and it seemed like the connection might have been broken. But then I finally heard him, loud and clear. I knew immediately that it was him, really him. That made me happy despite the fact that he was annoyed, which I could tell right away. Unless he was just busy? At any rate, it seemed like whatever he'd been occupied with had turned into something a bit more involved since the last time we'd spoken.

I said it was me again, and that I simply wanted to clarify things, as far as whether or not he'd be able to come by and fix the oven, because, as things stood, he didn't really need to worry about it. It could wait, of course. I said I was sure I had other ways of solving the problem. In fact, he really didn't need to come at all. I told him it had been quite silly of me to call him in the first place.

To my surprise, because he saw I wasn't expecting anything from him now, he apologized for his behavior on the telephone. He explained that he hadn't meant to be so curt, and then he even told me the reason he'd been so eager to get off the phone. He was being let go, as they say, from his duties as superintendent here in our building. He'd only found out a couple of days ago. And he hadn't been given any particular reason for this. Further, his employers had made it perfectly clear that it would be best if he found a new place to live as soon as possible. He apologized again but said that he couldn't really help me. He already had more than enough to do trying to find a place to stay for next week. And besides, it wasn't his responsibility anymore.

Before I could stop and think about what I was doing, I offered him Edwin's room. The room was rather large, with a dresser and bed, a window facing the courtyard, and would come with full kitchen and bathroom privileges. We could work out the monthly rent later, I added generously. Later I reprimanded myself for giving him so much leeway, but the truth was that I had no idea what a room like that was supposed to cost. I still haven't bothered to find out. But I didn't worry too much about it at the time. This was promising, I thought—the possibility of having someone else in the house. Such an unexpected opportunity. He didn't respond right away. Maybe he was a little confused, or at least caught off guard. As for me, well, I was impressed by my own quick thinking. I had seized an opportunity at the very same moment fate had dropped it into my lap. The super seemed to be thinking it over very carefully, weighing all of the pros and cons. At the same time, there was never any doubt as to the eventual outcome. His situation didn't really allow him much room for hesitation. Yes, thank you very much, he said finally. He would be very glad to accept my offer, at least until he found something else. He said that we should see how things went before making a more formal arrangement. I was happy. That was exactly how I would have put it myself. He needed a day to pack and clean up. He didn't have very many things, he said, certainly no more than would fit into a single room. We agreed that he would come by early the next morning, and that I would have the room all ready by eight o'clock.

After I hung up the telephone, I said, "Well, why not?" I wanted to make it all seem a bit less serious than—as I saw once I'd thought it over—it actually was. Serious or not, I began to worry unnecessarily. I told myself no great commitment had been made. I could toss him out the door whenever I wanted to. His situation was already difficult. He'd reconciled himself to the idea that he had to move. My offer had been entirely unexpected. He was hardly in a position to demand the world. We could sit down together and work out some kind of temporary arrangement, if necessary. He could stay for a week or two, and I would be free to say whether or not I thought things were working out. For his part, he would be perfectly free to go if he didn't like it here. Or free to stay if we were both happy with the situation.

I think it'll be good to have him here, with his practical know-how, his handiness. If something breaks, he'll be able to fix it right away. He knows how to do things like that. I could get him to make a folding screen . . . put up some shelves in the bathroom . . . I'll take care of the food, which I'm used to, and he'll make sure that everything is working like it should. And if he isn't too busy, we could have dinner together. It would be lovely to have someone to talk to again. It makes meals into something more than just an occasion to stuff our faces until we're full. Not that we'll sit there talking each other's ears off. We could simply make the occasional remark about something and know that we'd get a civil word in reply. I could even start to vary what I cook. Naturally I would begin to put more thought into the meals I'd make, since I would have someone to share them with. Naturally too he'll take care of the shopping. I'll have to let Sigri know that I don't need her anymore. It'll be a relief to tell her that. And she'll undoubtedly be thrilled not to have to bother with us anymore. I agree with Edwin. There's something untrustworthy about her. Her manner. She's the sort of person who'd just walk away with your money if you gave her the wrong change, rather than try to clear up the misunderstanding. She's never really put her heart and soul into the errands I send her on. On the contrary, she's always seemed a little annoyed. So I've never felt comfortable asking her to take care of anything special for us. I just gave her the same list every week, barring a few small changes when necessary. With the super living here, things will be different. I could even send him out on an extra trip if there's something we need, or if I decide to cook something special on a particular night. The store isn't far away, and it's open late. I could make a cake, if we wanted. I could just send him out with a list. I think I'll make a cake tomorrow, for when he moves in. I'll see if I can find a really good recipe for a cake. Then he could take a trip to the store after he's done settling in. That way, we could have a little celebration in the evening. His first evening here.

I thought about the meals I used to have with Edwin back when he was healthy. I remembered that funny little feeling I used to get, as if we were doing something utterly unprecedented, the two of us, sitting there day after day, at the same table. I could never quite get it into my head that that was the way things were supposed to be. It was always the same: first Edwin said nothing, just eating his food in silence. Then, halfway through the meal, once he was feeling less hungry, he leaned back in his chair, wiped his mouth with his napkin, and put his hands on the table, making a strange wriggling motion with his fingers—as though scratching someone's back. Then he began to talk about work, how the day had gone, what tragedies had played themselves out, which idiotic regulations he'd had to find a way to circumvent. He came home at the same time every day. He was always precise unless there was something special going on. I'd gotten into the habit of watching for him when it was getting close to five o'clock. I preferred to see him coming before I heard him at the door—though I never told him that I used to stand there at the window and follow him with my eyes. I don't think it would have been the same if he'd known he was being watched—there was something peaceful about him, I thought, when he came walking in . . . a dark figure, but always in an unflappable good mood, somehow. In summer, I'd see him as far away as the grassy stretch next to the train tracks. In winter, in the orange light, I'd only catch sight of him as he passed the playground. From there his route was as straight and invariable as a course plotted with a compass and chart. At last he disappeared—was gone for a second—until I heard him out in the entryway, real again. Every day, before I caught sight of him, I used to pretend that he wasn't ever coming home again—it seemed impossible that he would ever appear—and then it seemed like the great, wide, open space outside my window had a hard and unchangeable quality about it, like a prehistoric landscape. But then, there he was. When he was about halfway, passing our corner grocery, I turned off the burners on the stove, lifted off the kettles and pots, and put these on the kitchen table with trivets underneath—I associated the sight of him with food: meat patties, peas, carrots, potatoes, and dark sauces. I wonder, did this little mental game of mine help me to be more pleasant to him than I would have been otherwise, when he came home?

What will Edwin say? I'll have to tell him sooner or later. I should just come out and say it, tell him everything, plain and simple, that someone's going to move in here with us, that I've rented out his room, something I've been thinking about doing for many years. I've even mentioned it to him several times. I've told him I'd do it if the opportunity arose. He never had much to say on the subject. Maybe he never believed I really meant it. Well, now he'll see that I was serious. But there's no way I could bear to go in there just this moment. That's no place to be, with that awful light. I'll wait until morning when the super comes with his things, then I'll ask him to fix the light right away, before getting down to anything else . . . I'm almost looking forward to telling Edwin. I'm so excited about everything. I can't wait to see how it all goes. Maybe the super will stay. Maybe we'll get along really well. His name is Olav. Olav Martiniussen.

SWEETIE SAYS THAT the super, that horny fucker, has moved into our apartment . . . She gave him my old room . . . He was in here changing the bulb again, so she told me about it . . . She doesn't know how long he'll be here, she says that she hasn't come up with any concrete arrangements yet, she doesn't even know how much rent she's asking! Knowing her, she'll let him live here for next to nothing . . . and then, before she knows what hit her, she'll be paying him . . .

Afterward, she told me that my bag was full of blood this evening . . . did I detect a slight note of hope in her voice? I haven't felt any pain . . . Is it true that when you finally reach the end, you can't feel it coming?

I fart all the time, they just whistle right out of me, they're pretty quiet, but I can still hear them go, they break the silence, but they smell awful . . .

Does that kid realize what he's getting himself into?

They break silently, but smell violently. Ha! Don't come here and tell me that my farts don't still work like they should . . .

Maybe it's not really true about all that blood, maybe it was just something she said to distract me, to take my attention away from her and the super . . .

I tried to say something to her, but my jaws gotten so slack, it feels like it's just hanging there, dangling, which complicates things if I happen to want a piece of gum, which I do, I need one to quiet down the nausea . . . My intestines are churning like I ate a piece of bad meat or something . . . Like they want to push out into the air . . .
it feels like my lungs are going to leap out of my chest, they are pressing against my ribs, I can't catch my breath . . .

. . . it just pours out of me, a thick, sweet mush, bits of my ragged lungs . . .
. . . my esophagus, my windpipe, my tonsils, my uvula . . . everything . . .
my liver and my kidneys . . .
and my heart too, it's come loose and is on its way up . . . my stomach, like a rotten peapod, is all that's left, still gurgling on, all by itself . . . only thing to do is cough that up too . . .
. . . my bowels, my bowels are like a slithering snake . . .
. . . but someone's helping me, pulling them out of me, pushing and pulling . . .

Those two are a bad combination. They fan each other's flames . . . He's no better than she is . . . What makes a man agree to an arrangement like that? And how does he manage without ever coming in here? Of course, she must be letting him piss in the sink, so he can avoid the awkwardness of being here with me . . . that cunt. Does she realize what she's doing? But he won't be able to hold out forever . . . To begin with, he'll be as quiet as he can, so quiet that I almost won't hear him . . . I'll have to ask, "Is that you, Erna?" I'll hear the rustling and shuffling around, and if no one answers me, I'll know it's him . . . He'll feel a certain amount of respect for me, though he won't say anything on this first encounter . . . He'll feel like I am giving him an audience,

absolutely, and it won't be hard for me to pick up on the way he'll
be holding himself in contempt when he comes into my domain
. . . how he looks down on himself every time he comes in, every
time he feasts his eyes on me, the king . . .

He won't smell so bad either, at first . . . There will be a new
aroma at last, maybe even a refreshing one, though it's impossible
to predict . . . I admit that I've been longing to have someone
else's smell besides Sweetie's in here . . . I'll sit and sniff the air
gratefully after he's closed the door behind him . . .

Gradually, though, he'll start to feel more and more at home here,
and finally he won't worry about anything, he'll come busting
in here just like she does, Sweetie will tell him to act as though
there's no one here, goddamn it, and I'll bet after a while he
even starts to smell the same as her. No doubt about it, she'll be
stuffing the same things into him as she stuffs into herself, they'll
start having all of their meals together, they'll be together all the
time, and God only knows what kind of shit they'll be eating . . .
Finally it won't be possible to tell them apart, when one of them
creeps in here I won't even know which one I'm dealing with,
whether it's the one I've been married to for all of my adult life,
or the one who only moved in a few weeks ago . . .

there's a rustling in the gum wrappers, and I don't know who's
causing it . . .

there's a shuffling over by the mirror, and I don't know who it
is . . . someone comes, unlocks the window, and pushes the sash
up with a quick shove . . .

someone's standing there sneering at me, and I don't know who
it is . . .

I don't want to risk yelling for Sweetie, in case he's the one who
answers . . .

In the end, they'll start sneaking in here together, hand in hand,
barely managing to keep straight faces. They'll help each other's
clothes off and take a steamy bath, making it impossible to breathe

in here . . . I'll inhale the steam with his and her filth in it, filling
my lungs with the dead skin coming off their bodies . . .
Look, they can do whatever the hell they want, as long as they
leave me in peace . . . I've got nothing more to say on the matter,
everything's behind me, I'm finished with it, I'm just waiting for
him to decide, I mean the one who'll take me, I hope he does it
quickly but gently . . .
No, there won't be any problems, either for me or for the super,
why should there be, it's obvious what he has in mind, it was
the only way they could work it out, the only way they could
solve it, they planned everything out, they've been planning it
together from the very beginning, presumably the ambulance
is already on its way here at this very moment, and soon they'll
come stamping in here and lift me out of my chair, soon I'll be
carried out by strong arms and then placed in a room I've never
seen, surrounded by people I don't know, a hell, a den of
vipers . . . It would be easier if they just gave me an overdose of
morphine and had done with it . . .
They break silently, but smell violently. Ha! I'm ready. But I'll show
them. I'll die before they manage to carry out their plan . . .

Sweetie is worried. She hovers around me, then kneels down to
check for some sign of life . . .
I have to say, I'm enjoying this . . .
She can beg and whimper as much as she wants to, but I won't
move a muscle . . .
I feel fine . . .
For the first time in ages, I feel absolutely fine . . .
I sit absolutely still, pretending I'm dead, and in any case, it won't
be terribly long before that's more or less the truth . . .

What does she think she's doing?
She's stroking my cheek . . .

She's so upset . . .

Everything's so easy and peaceful now, it's quiet, they both went out together, they're walking hand in hand over the lawn, eating ice cream and talking about the weather . . .
It feels good to be alone. I feel nothing. I'm resting, my body is resting, everything is peaceful . . .
I think things are actually running a little slower up here now. Yes, they must be . . .
It's like a machine that's powering down . . .
My thoughts are quiet and chilly. They float by like tiny leeches . . .
I don't move a muscle. I sit here with my head completely at peace. I've sat in this position for several hours now, several days for all I know, maybe even weeks, all without moving my head, without so much as cracking a smile, without opening my eyes even once . . . My skeleton is the chair I sit in . . .

Someone should be here. You ought to have someone with you when it happens, right? If not, you forfeit your right to a good parting scene . . . I should have thought of that before . . .
But I am not alone. I have Sweetie of course. Not just her, but the super now too. I'm sure he'll be here when it happens. And he'll take care of Sweetie just like she's taken care of me. Maybe what she has done isn't so bad after all, when it comes right down to it. Now, there are two of them here to look after me, to take care of practical matters, to help clean up after me, after I'm gone, to remove all trace of me, and wash everything clean. Sweetie always has my best interests at heart. She guards me like a treasure. She looks after everything . . . She'll never leave me. Not now when she knows that the end is approaching . . .
Approaching Edwin. Edwin Mortens . . .

This could be the last thought I think. I should hurry up and make a list of last wishes . . .

What should I concentrate on? What sort of thing is suitable for one's final moments? No, I don't remember anything anymore . . . I've forgotten everything. But that's what I wanted of course, that everything should disappear . . .

I guess maintaining one's memory requires a certain strength, and I've lost that strength now, I don't remember anything, it's a completely blank slate up here, I can't manage to keep anything in my head beyond whatever it is I happen to be thinking about at the moment . . . No, it's all gone. I've managed to reach my goal, to forget everything. But is it true? Have I managed to do it? Has everything really been forgotten? Am I sure? It certainly feels like it . . .

Where are my shoes? Has she given them to him? Yes, she'll probably give him everything in my closet . . .

I really wish she was here now. How does she manage to stay away? It's that horny bastard who keeps her from coming. He knows damn well what he's doing. She lets herself be deceived. Are they just sitting out there waiting for it all to be over? Listening carefully for the old fucker to kick the bucket? Haven't they considered cracking the door open, just to double check, to listen for breathing, to hear how quiet it's gotten in here? Well, there isn't anything to hear anyway . . .

Are they just waiting for the ambulance men to come in and take me away?

I'd like her here with me one more time before it's over. I want to speak to her one more time before I go. Then, he can have her, let him have her, let him do whatever the hell he wants with her . . .

I've thought about taking back everything I've ever said to her, if she comes in to see me . . . I'll delete everything, I never meant any of it anyway, it's all just been an ugly, unhinged fabrication on my part, every bit of it . . . I'll tell her that, and I'll make sure she hears me, I'll ask her to forget all about it, which I know she's good at doing. I don't want there to be anything left to bother her after I'm gone . . . She's my wife, after all . . . Above all, she's my wife . . .

Where is she? What are they doing?

What's he doing to delay her? I let a fart slip out. It might be my last. It puffs into the bag and makes me think of the blood again . . .

OLAV SHOWED UP this morning with his things—he ran up and down and up and down the stairs—it didn't take him more than six or seven trips, and then everything was done. I couldn't tell what it all was for, since everything was packed up in black bags—though I also saw him bring in the yellow bag from his first visit. He can't have much else besides clothing. I've thought about asking if I could wash his things for him, at least at first, until he settles into his new surroundings and routine. He brought a new fluorescent tube for the bathroom right away—he's still the superintendent for a few more days. I mentioned to him that the bulb he put in last time had been too strong—or, to be precise, too white. I said that I'd be happier with something a little dimmer, though preferably of the same basic type, if that was possible. He told me he would see what he could find. It didn't seem like it was any trouble at all for him. It was exactly like I'd imagined: the two of us doing small favors for each other the best we can.

Later, I took him into the kitchen, showed him around, and instructed him in the use of various kitchen apparatuses. I told him that it would be best if he familiarized himself with everything right away—then, he could do things on his own later on without having to depend on me. I showed him the dishwasher, the stove, the coffee maker, and the toaster, and I even found the little gadget that you can use to make grilled-cheese sandwiches, which has been sitting there and gathering dust and which I've never even tried. But with him in the house, maybe I'll finally use it . . . or maybe he will . . . I suggested that he try out the coffee machine right away, so I could watch how he did things and correct him if he did anything wrong, and then we could sit down with a nice cup of coffee afterwards. He said something in reply that I didn't quite understand, though it was clear that he didn't want any coffee just then. I'd thought to ask him if there was anything special he might want for dinner, but now I couldn't get myself to do it. I was sure it would end in a misunderstanding, though I'm not sure which of us I was more worried about. He opened the refrigerator and looked over its contents. Judging by the look on his face, it seemed as though he hadn't expected to find much. He surprised me. I'd expected him to be more timid on his first day here as a tenant. There were a number of things I wanted to make him aware of, but now I couldn't remember any of it. I didn't know what to say. He took a banana from the basket on the counter, peeled it, took a bite, and made a face. Then he folded the peel back and replaced what was left of the banana in the basket. He looked around a bit restlessly, like he was expecting something to happen. I didn't know what to say. "Excuse me," he said, "there's something I have to go fix." He stretched his arm out into the air, making the sleeve of his jacket slide back over his watch, which emerged like a set of glistening teeth in a predator's mouth. Then he smoothed his hair back with the extended hand. I saw a scornful twitch around his mouth. I almost didn't recognize him. It was like he'd changed into a completely different person in the space of a moment, and I couldn't help but think: So, this is what he's really like.

And then he left. We hadn't had time to talk about anything.

Does he think that he can just come and go as he pleases? And now I remembered all the things I should have said, things that we had to settle as quickly as possible. If not, we'd have problems before we knew it, and the last thing I want is to get tangled up in some kind of conflict with him. There isn't really very much I can do if he starts making trouble right off the bat. If he says he wants a key of his own, I'll say no—until we've settled on a few ground rules, I'll keep the only key. The onus is on him to make this arrangement work, not me. Why didn't I work this all out before he moved in? I can't ask him to leave when he's only just arrived. If nothing else, I feel I need to give him a chance. Of course, one chance is all some people need to roll right over you. Maybe Edwin was right. When you get right down to it, maybe the super is just as shameless as everyone else out there. Maybe he's trying to put one over on me, with his easygoing manner, his friendliness. Maybe he's already come up with a scheme to get the upper hand with me. I think I've made up my mind. I'll let him stay here a week, two at the most. That's no more than I promised him. Then he can get going. I'm sure it won't be a problem for him. This way he'll be able to find a place that actually suits him. He said so himself, he doesn't need a lot of room. He doesn't own any more than he can carry himself. I'll tell Edwin my plan and see what he thinks. If I run into problems, maybe Edwin can talk to Olav for me. Edwin is hardly defenseless. I'm sure he'd know just how to frighten the boy, if Olav tried anything. I'll go in and tell him everything. I should do it now, before it's too late. Then I'll know I'm not alone, if a situation develops. I'm sure Edwin would defend me if he found out that the super was trying to hurt me in some way. Oh, damn it. How could I let myself be taken in by someone like Olav? Someone who only ever thinks of himself? Who just wants to take advantage of everyone? And I'd just made the decision on a whim, rashly, without giving it any thought, without consulting Edwin . . . it made me feel sick.

And now something else occurred to me, something really terrifying: What if this situation was exactly what would finally finish
Edwin off? That I'd opened our door for this self-righteous . . .
arrogant . . . brazen . . . selfish . . . inconsiderate superintendent
. . . Yes, I thought—and I don't know which was worse, the fear
or the guilt—it wouldn't be at all surprising to find that, in the
end, it was nothing more than my own thoughtlessness that killed
Edwin Mortens.

A salesman came by today while Olav was out—at first I thought
it was him, but after I opened the door, I realized I was looking at
a complete stranger. My first impulse was to close the door again
without saying anything, but it was already too late, he knew
exactly how to talk his way in—of course, that's what they learn in
their training, how to not take no for an answer. He had a couple
of suitcases with him along with a few cardboard boxes. He also
had a tall, white vacuum cleaner that looked quite futuristic. He
set all his things out on the carpet in the living room and began
opening all the suitcases and boxes one at a time. It was like he
was in his own home, like he did this every day. I tried to get a
word in edgewise and explain that I wasn't interested regardless of
what he had to show me, but he simply went on talking while he
screwed various attachments onto and off his vacuum cleaner. He
looked like a little boy, crawling back and forth across my carpet.
Then he stood up and began to pull on the vacuums hose,
which was suddenly three times as long, and before I knew it,
he started to vacuum the ceiling. A small black nozzle at the
end of a telescopic tube waved around in the air over my head.
A moment later, he began vacuuming the walls. He even went
over to the window frame and vacuumed that too. He held the
attachment in one hand and supported his lower back with the
other . . . I think he was trying to show me that a person could
use this vacuum cleaner without ever having to bend over. Then

he changed the large nozzle for a small, and began working on one of the chairs. Bubbles began to form in the seat, and soon the chair was covered in foam. Next, he turned off the vacuum cleaner and checked his watch. I was afraid that his demonstration was over, that I would have to sign a sales contract before he was willing to clean the foam off of my chair, that this was his way of breaking down people's resistance to his pitch.

He left and then was gone for a while, though all of his equipment was still on my floor, so I knew he'd have to reappear soon. I have no idea why he went away. Maybe it's something they do to give people time to think things over or discuss things with their families before they decide whether to make a purchase or not ... For my part, I just stood there, waiting for him to come back.

When he did, he had another cardboard box with him. He produced ten to fourteen discs from inside, which he displayed neatly on the coffee table. The discs all had tiny feet underneath. He explained how all these accessories worked together. After that, he considered himself finished. He smiled broadly, looked at his watch again, then looked at me expectantly. I mentioned the foam in the chair. He acted like he'd forgotten all about it, but I am quite sure he hadn't. He went to the chair—a bit sulkily, it seemed—and attached another gadget to the vacuum cleaner. When he was finished, there wasn't so much as a pearl of foam left: the seat cushion looked like it had been freshly washed, or anyway as close to being washed as it'd ever been. He packed up his things. I told him that I managed very well with the equipment I already had, but he still wanted to leave his papers, brochures, and card with me, and he stuck these into my hand. I think there were at least five or six different methods of payment I could have chosen. Strangely enough, he didn't seem at all disappointed when he left. More like he would have been flabbergasted if I'd actually bought something from him. I'm sure most of his potential customers greeted him with abuse and suspicion. I told him that if my old vacuum cleaner—which had run like clockwork for twenty-five years—ever broke down, I would be sure to purchase exactly the model he had demonstrated to me.

After he left, I laid down on the sofa. He had been here for almost an hour, talking the whole time. I rested there for a while with my arm across my forehead. I found myself drifting off to sleep. I didn't dare close my eyes, or I wouldn't be able to sleep that night. I noticed that there were white stripes on the ceiling where the salesman had vacuumed. I realized that I would have to wash everything down, so it wouldn't look ugly. Maybe I could get Olav to do it. Washing the ceiling is hard work, suitable for a young man. Where did Olav get to, by the way? He hasn't been here all day. What will he do if the weather turns bad? There was a rumble of thunder then, startling me, rattling the windowpanes. It began to rain. For a moment, I wasn't sure where I was. I felt as though I'd woken up in a different place. The living room seemed smaller, drier, warmer, a little world of its own.

I felt a pain in my heart when I stood up. I had to sit down again, and I pressed my hand against my chest as hard as I could. I thought that it might ease the pain, somehow—and it did. The pain finally went away entirely, fading like a distant sound. I thought: I haven't eaten regularly for a while now. I'm becoming just like him. Maybe that's why this happened. My stomach makes little mouse-like noises. Maybe I ought to be more worried than I am. I don't know. Mostly, I worry about Edwin. I can't remember when he last made a sound. He doesn't move and just sits there with his face turned away to the wall, like he doesn't want us to see him. His food was lying untouched in his lap as usual the last time I thought to bring him something. I can't remember when that was. I wish he would scream for his life or something. I'd give anything to hear him yelling at me again. I wish he was angry at me, furious about something that I didn't understand, accusing me, nagging me about something or other, some little, insignificant thing.

It's really raining hard. I see the light from the corner grocery's sign smudging off onto the windowpane, flowing out in big blisters. The benches out there all look like they've tipped over. The lilacs along the path lie flat against the ground. Every once in a while they straighten up a bit before the wind flattens them again. Usually there are people walking by in the evenings, crossing the lawn to enter one of the houses. Now there isn't a soul. As though they're too fragile for the bad weather. Besides, I've always thought there was something suspicious about people who walk alone in the evening. When I was younger, I always tensed up a little whenever I walked past one of them. I always expected the worst. But in this kind of weather, no one goes walking. Not even Olav. What's keeping him so long? Is it the rain? Maybe I'll spot him as he arrives . . . I'll suggest that we institute a system whereby he'll always let me know approximately when he plans to be home if he's going to be out for most of the day. If I don't know this in advance, I won't be able to concentrate on anything but waiting for him, and it'll be impossible for me to get any rest before he comes back.

There's somebody running now. Is it him? Yes, it's Olav. He's wearing the cap with the visor again. But I didn't think he had that with him when he left this morning. Someone told me once that it doesn't help to run. You get just as wet running as you do walking. He's holding a bag. Why is he running across the lawn if he's heading for our stairway? No, he's running past it, at an angle, full speed ahead. Has he forgotten the number of our apartment? What's he doing? It must be something terribly important for him to have gone out in this weather in the first place. And he isn't even properly dressed. He's just wearing the same blue jacket he had on the first time he came to the apartment.

There, he's disappeared into the little shelter that houses the bicycle stands. The sheets of corrugated metal are shaking. One corner's come loose—opening and shutting like a mouth. It looks like the whole thing could be ripped apart and strewn over the yard at any moment.

Not a sound from the bathroom. The silence makes me so uneasy. The weather's gotten colder, recently. We don't have any mittens in the house, so I've pulled a pair of old cotton socks over his hands, so he won't freeze. Good God. Today's been so strange already, it wouldn't surprise me at all if it was the day . . . the day it happened. As though everything that's happened so far happened just to prepare me. I'm afraid. No. It won't happen today. I'm sure of it. It would feel like an insult. I'm not ready. Some other day, yes, but not today. It wouldn't be like him, to leave me like that. With a stranger in the house. I remember I dreamed once that I was dead and could see him sitting there, worrying, crying. He sat in his chair and sobbed like a child. It was a good dream. And when I woke up, everything was perfectly clear to me. I felt I finally understood something.

Afterward, though, I couldn't remember what this something was. I find I've always taken it for granted that he'd be the one to go first, even though there's no real reason for me to think so. I've been putting a little money aside every month for the funeral. It's been comforting to watch my savings grow, through the years. Every time I've slipped a rubber band around a new bundle of bills, it's felt like a solemn act, a respectful gesture, even though it was secret. I've got enough saved up now for both our funerals. Nothing would be worse than being broke on the day we disappear. I found De-Sarg's IOU when I straightened up Edwin's room before Olav moved in. It was in the top drawer of the dresser, along with paperclips, rolls of scotch tape, Edwin's old tools, and a yellow sheet of paper with Kronsæther's letterhead and an illegible signature, wooly with dust. But I left it all there. Edwin doesn't talk about any of it anymore. If he doesn't remember it, he won't have any use for it. We won't see each other in the hereafter. That much I know. We won't see each other anywhere. I believe—we both believe—that when it's over, it's over. The days will seem so long when Edwin isn't here anymore. What will I do to fill them? I have never been alone before. I remember so little about the days when we were first together. I wish I'd kept some notes. That's something you never think about until you need it, and by the time you need it, it's too late. We never bought a camera. Edwin said several times that he would, but it never came to anything. We never took a single picture. The only one we have is of Edwin with the Kronsæther staff the year he took over. He looks so handsome in his white coat. It suited him—so much I used to wish he wore it at home too. Maybe if he'd had some other suitable jackets, I would remember the young Edwin better. Or maybe it would have been easier for me to hold onto my memories if I hadn't had to care for him all alone, all this time. I've seen him every single day, from then till now. All the changes happened so slowly that I didn't notice any of them. It'll be awfully quiet here without him. But it's awfully quiet even now. There hasn't been a sound from the bathroom for ages. At least I haven't heard anything. It almost seems like he's already gone. It's after nine o'clock. I think I'll check on him now.

STIG SÆTERBAKKEN (1966–2012) was one of Norway's most acc-laimed and controversial authors, translators, and essayists.

STOKES SCHWARTZ's translation work includes technical, histo-rical, and literary pieces. He studied Scandinavian languages and literature at the University of Wisconsin-Madison, the University of Minnesota, and the Norwegian University of Science and Technology in Trondheim.